1

When Ray Richmond announced he was moving to Hollywood, Pastor Adams proclaimed, "You're eighteen, you have no idea the sort of things that go on there."

Raymond had a fairly good idea. After all, this was 1925. Those "sort of things" was one of the reasons he wanted to go to the modern day Sodom and Gomorrah. "I've had enough of Iowa."

"But son, I..."

Ray cut him off. "I need to make my place in the world." Pastor Adams and his wife had been nice enough to become his legal guardians after his parents died. Despite his gratitude, Ray still bristled when the Pastor called him son.

The Pastor bowed his head. "But to go *there*..."

Ray remained firm in his resolve to leave. "Pastor, I'm grateful for everything you and Mrs. Adams have done, but something else is calling me, something more than corn fields and dairy cows." Ray was determined to make a name for himself. He didn't say so. That would be wasted breath. The Pastor would never understand his need to be famous.

The Pastor rubbed the back of his neck. "Ray, I know it hasn't always been easy for you here."

Ray smirked. That was an understatement. The folks of Reeversville had made it abundantly clear time and again he was the offspring of a couple of outcasts, a Jew and a Catholic, a Christ killer and a Papist. That was mighty notable in the mostly Protestant county. The town folk had shunned his family from the day they moved into town.

After his parents died during the big blizzard five years ago, only Ray, the Pastor, and his wife had attended the funeral. Ray made up his mind then and there, one day he was going to make every one of the townsfolk regret their behavior. *One day they will sit up and take notice of Ray Richmond*. The time had come to make good on that declaration.

Two years ago, Ray found out something about himself when a traveling salesman came through town. He'd been selling cloth. They spread one of his fabric samples out on the ground and fornicated in a cornfield. The salesman said there were places where doing what they did was just a part of life.

Mrs. Adams wept when she heard that Ray was leaving. No argument, just tears. She considered Ray to be her boy. She and the Pastor had never been blessed with children of their own. She took the two hundred dollars she kept in a jar above the stove and pushed it into Ray's hand. "Be careful out there, and let us know how your doing," she had said.

The Matinee Idol © 2017 Owen Keehnen

Published by Out Tales Publishing

Cover Art by Adrian Nicholas

The Matinee Idol

By Owen Keehnen

Ray answered "I will" even though he had no intention of doing so. Once he left this godforsaken town, he was going to become someone else. He had nothing here worth remembering, but Ray was grateful for the money.

His potential was being wasted in Reeversville. Every time he looked in the mirror these past two years, the handsome young man in the reflection would whisper, "What are you doing with your life?" He knew he was just as good looking as some of those fellows up on the silver screen. Hollywood was where be belonged.

Two days later he was on the train bound for Los Angeles. Ray smiled. His real life was about ready to begin.

*****

Brick stood in the middle of the pasture and looked out at the wide arc of Montana sky.
He couldn't deny its majestic beauty. He loved the grandeur of mountains.

Brick turned. His Pa was galloping Thunder across the field toward him. This would not be good. "Damn it boy, get your fool head out of the clouds. Quit your daydreaming."

"Sorry Pa," Brick said. Pa was drunk again, but Brick was hard pressed to recall a day when his Pa had stayed sober until sunset. He knew from experience where the day was headed.

Brick knew Pa's disgusted look. He'd received it more days than not. His Pa grumbled as he rode back across the field. Brick didn't need to hear the specifics. He'd been called a stupid giant and an oaf often enough. Usually the comment came with a whack on the side of the head. Sometimes more. "I used to think it was a blessing having a son as big as you, but what you got in size you lack in smarts."

Brick wasn't stupid. He just didn't say all that he was thinking. His Ma knew that, but his Pa never saw it at all. Ma said the booze blinded him to it. "Blinds him to a lot of things," she added.

Brick's Pa didn't know the first thing about him and didn't seem too interested to learn.
Brick loved to paint. Mostly the mountains. Sometimes an animal. When his Pa saw him settling up an easel in the barn, he'd broken it to bits and used it for kindling.

"It ain't manly for a boy to be drawing," he said, throwing the bits of wood onto the fire. Drunk again.

Brick had hidden his drawing pad ever since. He worked with wood in front of his Pa. Woodworking seemed to be manly enough.

Brick knew the kind of son his Pa had wanted to have. He was not that son. There wasn't much more to discuss than that. He was never going to be good enough in his Pa's bloodshot eyes, and he was tired of being called an idiot. He thought about leaving and dreamed about what lay beyond those hills.

That night he pulled his Ma aside. I can't live under this roof with him."

All she said was, "I know." She gave him a hug and told him not to marry the first woman he met. Brick promised her he wouldn't.

He slipped out the next day before sunrise.

The back steps creaked, and his Pa was up in a flash. Brick said he was leaving. His Pa called him a fool and said he wasn't going anywhere. When his Pa drew back to punch him, Brick slugged him in the gut. He didn't want to do it. Pa had left him no choice. Anyone could see that.

Once his Pa caught his breath, Brick heard him shouting from the back porch. "Good riddance. Just know right now you are never coming back. Never! You'll find it ain't so easy out there, boy. You'll find out a lot of things."

When Brick turned, he saw his Ma standing behind his Pa. Even from a distance, he could see the tears in her eyes. He wished he could take her with him. He swore one day he would go back for her.

Once he got to the main road, a man in a motor car pulled over and offered him a ride.

2

Ray loved Los Angeles from the moment he arrived in town. The city was just as he pictured it—big and sprawling, with fruit you could pick right off the tree. He found a place to stay and starting looking through the trade papers for movie work. He heard that was how you did it.

Ray had only been in town a few days when he received his first invitation. Theodore, a resident at the rooming house where Ray was staying, saw the handsome broad-shouldered young man sitting on the back porch looking through *Variety* and invited him to a party. "There's a shindig at one of the beach houses down in Long Beach. Did you want to tag along? Never know who you're going to meet. There's bound to be industry people there."

"You think so?" Ray had asked. Making some contacts sounded like a good career plan. He knew for a fact that a lot of folks got their break that way.

"I know so." Theodore put a hand on his shoulder and let it linger.

Ray was no fool. He knew what that touch meant, but he wasn't interested in messing around with Theodore. Ray knew the easiest way to avoid the situation was to play dumb.

The following night, Theodore and Ray hopped into a Studebaker driven by Morgan, one of Theodore's friends. Morgan worked in the offices at Vitagraph. Ray knew what kind of friend Morgan was to Theodore, but he acted naive once again. Morgan broke out a flask as soon as they hopped in the car.

Theodore took a swig. "That is some fine brown plaid." He looked at Ray. "That's bootleg whiskey for those who don't know the lingo."

Morgan handed the flask to Ray. "Coffin varnish?"

Ray took a drink to be polite. The whiskey burned his throat. Morgan brushed his hand against his thigh. Ray put his hands in his lap to block its advance. Morgan turned to Theodore. "I thought you said he was a live wire."

Theodore shook his head. Just because Ray liked men did not mean he liked *all* of them. They could not get to Long Beach fast enough for Ray.

The group could hear the music from the road. As they swung through the front gates and cruised up the winding drive to the house. Morgan slicked back his shiny hair and Theodore did the same. By then, Ray had made it abundantly clear he wasn't interested in any sort of whoopee with either Morgan or Theodore or both. Those two disappeared as soon as they entered the party, and Ray feared he might have to find another way to get back to Los Angeles.

The hooch was flowing freely, and the music was deafening.All the furniture had been pushed aside in the main room. All around, couples were cutting a rug. Sheiks and shebas, flappers and palookas, high hats and gold diggers, and gigolos and Janes galore. Couples leaned over the upstairs balcony and shouted to those on the dance floor. Couples were necking everywhere. The scent of marijuana was in the air.

This shindig was unlike anything Ray had ever seen in Iowa. The decadence of it, the excess and excitement, the crazed pace thrilled him. But he still felt out of place, like an observer. Aloof. Stiff. Maybe he just needed some of that bootleg booze to loosen up. As if on cue, a waiter came by with a tray of drinks. Ray took one. This was much smoother stuff than the horse liniment Morgan had offered him in the car.

"Careful, one will do ya and two will undo ya," winked a flapper as she breezed by.

With a drink in hand, Ray felt less out of place. He scanned the crowd but didn't recognize anyone famous. He saw a cowboy across the room. The gent was handsome as hell in a rugged sort of way, and a tall drink of water. He stood a good head above the crowd. Ray couldn't help but stare. The cowboy looked around and tried to smile, but mostly he kept his head bowed. A wallflower. A real cancelled stamp. Ray knew how he felt. Ray was going to introduce himself a moment later, but the cowboy was gone.

Ray didn't want to seem like a flat tire, but mingling wasn't easy with this crowd. The party had started early in the afternoon and by the time he had arrived everyone was ossified or petting or engaged in a closed conversation.

Ray took another drink and wandered out to the balcony. He could hear the roar of the ocean. The strong breeze smelled of salt. When he turned away from the wind to light a cigarette, he saw the cowboy out on the balcony as well. Legs crossed. Leaning against the railing. Even sexier in the shadows. The light from the moon cut the angles on his face.

Ray turned to him. "The ocean sure is something, isn't it?"

The man nodded.

"My name is Ray," he said, extending his hand.

"I'm Brick," he replied in a deep voice.

Ray felt a tingle at the strength of the cowboy's grip. "I don't know anybody here, and most of them seem otherwise occupied. Maybe I just need to catch up. Everyone in there sure has a snootful."

"I'm here because I helped build the pool." Brick tilted his head towards the construction on the side of the house. "Lady of the house invited me."

"Wow, the ocean in your backyard, and you still need a pool. Now that's living," laughed Ray. He eyed Brick more closely. Broad shoulders, six-four, muscular build, light brown hair, strong jaw, and those gorgeous brown eyes. Brick's sex appeal grabbed him by the lapels and shook him. This man took his breath away. Ray suspected he knew exactly why the lady of the house had invited him. Ray put down his cocktail. "I've never been swimming in the ocean."

Brick smiled. He had dimples as well. "Never?"

"No, I only got into Hollywood this week. This is as close as I've been to the Pacific."

"There's a flight of stairs here if you want to get closer."

"Care to join me?" Ray asked.

Brick kicked back from his leaning pose on the deck and followed Ray down the stairs.

"Is that what you do? Work construction."

"That's what I'm doing since I got to Los Angeles a couple months back. Good money in construction. Lots of folks are building."

"They're calling Hollywood and the surroundings a real boom town. You work building for any movie people?"

Brick thought for a moment. "I helped build a butler's room above Nita Naldi's garage."

"Oh, she's terrific. I just saw her with Valentino in *Cobra*. Did you get a chance to meet her?"

Brick shook his head. "She was away making a movie someplace."

Ray looked down and laughed. Brick's boots were not ideal for walking in the sand. "Looks like you're having problems with those boots, cowboy. I'm taking off my shoes. I want to feel the sand on my feet."

Brick did the same. "Are you in pictures? he asked.

"I aim to be."

"And I bet you'll make it, too."

The two headed towards the surf and began walking along the shoreline. Ray liked the feel of his feet digging into the moist sand. The waves licked at their ankles. The music and voices from the party still cut through the sound of the Pacific. The moon hung above the water, the reflection glazing the surface.

"Sure looks inviting, don't it."

Brick nodded.

Ray began to unbuckle his pants. "Want to take a quick dip with me."

Brick blushed and said he only had skivvies on under his pants.

"Me too," said Ray. "We're just two guys," he added, already unbuttoning his pants and sliding them down his legs. His shirt came next.

With little hesitation, Brick began to undress.

As he stared at Brick stripping down, a jolt moved down Ray's body and into his boxers. Stunning. The man was perfect in every way. To cover his growing excitement, Ray ran into the surf. Brick followed. The two frolicked and shouted a bit. The water was cold at first, but they soon grew used to it. Brick swam behind Ray. "What do you think?"

Ray turned around, surprised.

Brick laughed, "Of the ocean."

Ray laughed as well. He grabbed Brick around the shoulders and dunked him.

When Brick came to the surface a moment later, he flipped his hair back from his eyes. "Oh, yeah?"

Ray was already running towards the shore when Brick tackled him. The two wrestled in the shallow water. Grappling. Each feeling the power and exertion of the other, they strained and grunted. They laughed as they ran and tossed one another into the surf. Ray felt Brick's penis brush his thigh. *Swollen.* Contact was making them frisky. Ray was unable to control his excitement. He ran toward the shore. When Brick tackled him a final time, he rolled onto his side. Ray's erection ground into his thigh. Brick bent closer. Without thinking Ray leaned up and kissed him on the mouth. He had no idea what would happen, only what felt right. Brick returned his kiss. *Harder. Urgent.* They kissed again as Ray's hands began to explore Brick's body. Moving lower he noticed the helmet of Brick's member poking through the fly of his boxers. Ray wrapped a hand around it and reached inside for more. *Huge. Thick. Warm. Pulsing.* Brick began to move in Ray's hand. "Tighten your fist," Brick whispered.

Ray heard laughter on the porch. He couldn't tell if they were visible on the beach. Perhaps. The crowd was so bent and hoary-eyed, who knew if they'd even notice. The moon was awfully bright. Even if they were noticeable from the deck, Ray doubted this crowd knew the meaning of the word taboo, but thought it best not to take any chances.

Ray took Brick by the hand. Grabbing their clothes, they ran to an outcropping of rocks just up the beach where the sand was cooler. They could still hear the party. The rocks shielded them from view. Ray pulled Brick close and kissed him again. He tasted of salt and a slight sourness. He moved his mouth down Brick's chin and planted kisses along the sides of his neck. Brick slapped him on the behind. Ray tongued the nipples on Brick's broad chest. The cowboy's hand continued down Ray's back. Two fingers moved between the firm globes of Ray's behind and lingered at his hole. Circling. Ray's turn to moan. He pushed Brick's hand away and sank to his knees, kissing a treasure trail of hair down. Brick's huge erection jutted upward at a forceful angle.

Ray took Brick in his mouth. The girth caused him to gag. He wanted this so badly. Brick, his penis, the moment, all of it. Ray was ravenous. He relaxed his throat and eventually felt the head of Brick's manhood hit the back of his throat. Brick grabbed the sides of his head, thrusting gently, and then with more force. Greater urgency. Balls slapping Ray's chin. He grabbed Brick's nuts and held them in his hand, coated them with his tongue. Ray could tell Brick liked it by the slight buckling of his knees,. Ray pushed Brick back against the dark rocks. Cold. Sharp.

Ray sucked greedily. Brick moved forward a bit and said the stones were scraping his back. Eventually Ray eased him back again. By then Brick didn't seem to care about a few scratches. Ray knelt on shells. Pain provided a greater contrast to the pleasures.

Brick pulled Ray to his feet and kissed him. Ray wondered if Brick tasted himself on his lips. He wondered if Brick was eager to service him in the same way. The cowboy's actions seemed to say yes. He was already kissing down his body. Ray wondered if Brick had ever done this before. Ever thought about doing it. Did it matter? The cowboy was about to do it now. Brick knelt on the shells. Ray felt his long arms and calloused hands roam his body. He looked up with those big brown eyes. "You are so beautiful," Brick had said, so earnestly and with such tenderness Ray felt his heart skip a beat. Brick bent forward and began giving Ray's privates small kisses and licks. The crown of Ray's penis brushed his lips. "That's it," he said as Brick licked one side and then the other. Coating it with saliva. He gagged a bit as he slowly took Ray into his mouth. "Take your time, cover your teeth, that's right." Ray looked down at the gorgeous naked man servicing him. What Brick lacked in skill and experience, he made up for in enthusiasm. Ray was so aroused. He needed to pace himself.

Ray stopped Brick's sucking and told him to lay down away from the shells. Ray did the same so they were lying head to toe and toe to head. He'd seen a photo of this sex act on a French postcard. "This way we can please each other at the same time," he said. Each man took the other in their mouth on the cool damp sand. Ray smelled the citrus trees and the seaweed and the Indian hop cigarette someone was having on the balcony. He could hear the conversation clearly.

The first voice giggled, "He said I was full of pep and I asked him to show me how much he cared. Something I can take to the bank."

"Perfect-a-vous," squealed the other starlet.

"And voila, another bauble," added the first.

Ray found the thought of others being so near, so audible, made their lovemaking more exciting.

Both men sucked faster. anxious to give and get in equal measure. Brick reached around and manhandled Ray's ass again. Ray liked the feel of his hand there. So perfect and in control. Forceful. That was the sort of grip that did not let go easily. Brick gave each perfect orb a slap and took Ray even deeper into his mouth.

Ray felt Brick'a penis thicken and twitch. The cowboy was nearing orgasm. Ray was not far behind. Brick took Ray from his mouth and lay back on the sand. His features contorted. Brick stiffened as he released first, filling Ray's mouth with warm seed. Ray felt each blast hit the back of his throat. He had to focus to refrain from gagging. He wanted every drop of Brick's ejaculate.

A moment later, Ray was there himself. Ready to explode. He rose to is knees and moaned as he released onto Brick's furry chest. Brick looked up at him and smiled as he began to smear Ray's semen across his torso and stomach. He took a bit on his finger and brought it to his mouth. "I think there's some sand in there," he laughed.

Brick was full or surprises.

Different voices were on the balcony. One of them called, "Anyone down there?

Another voice shouted, "Hello?"

They ignored the voices. Both men lay spent for a moment on the cool sand. "God, that was fantastic." Ray finally said. Brick said nothing. Ray didn't know how to interpret his silence. He assumed it had been magical for him as well. Maybe he was wrong. He wondered once again if this had been Brick's first time with another man. Maybe he was conflicted. Filled with regret. Ray leaned closer to him. "Look, we can just pretend this never happened."

Brick turned to him. "I don't think I can. Some things there's no forgetting."

"Hey, what is going on over there," Came another shout from the deck. Ray heard a couple of people moving drunkenly down the stairs.

"Sounds like a party," the other voice laughed.

"Is there room for one or two more?"

"Or three," said another voice laughing.

The approaching voices giggled in unison. There was no ignoring the party-goers this time.

Ray and Brick grabbed their clothes and ran down the beach, attempting to keep to the shadows. A ways down, they washed themselves in the surf and ended up sleeping on the sand. Early the next morning, they walked up to the main road and hitchhiked back to Los Angeles.

3

Their ride dropped Ray and Brick off in town, near Brick's attic apartment in Hollywood. "Want to come over?" Brick asked.

Ray nodded. He'd like that a lot. His body ached and his skin tingled with how much he was looking forward to it.

Brick motioned to a place across the street and down the block. "That's where I am. The attic apartment of that building with the stairs on the side. I live alone," he added.

"Nice that you have your own entrance," Ray said nervously. He had to say something, anything. Ray was anxious to be with Brick again. He felt nervous like it was his first time. Judging from the bulge in his pants, Brick was eager for a replay of last night as well. "Is this place expensive?" When Brick told him the price, Ray was surprised. Less than he was paying at the rooming house across town.

"Usually this place goes for more, but my landlady, Mrs. Hanover, gives me a deal on account of my doing work around the place for her."

"That's nice."

"I think she's lonely." Brick unlocked the door. He motioned for Ray to enter. Ray felt his breath catch. There were butterflies in his stomach. He had to say something.

He asked about the furniture. Brick explained the place came furnished, so the mattress, dresser and side table all were Mrs. Hanover's. Ray looked toward the easel by the window. "And is that yours?"

Brick blushed. He said he bought the easel and some paints last week. "The first big splurge I've made since coming to town."

"I admire painters," said Ray.

Brick smiled. "Painting keeps me sane. Always has. When I'm not painting, something is going on."

Ray looked at the painting-in-progress on the easel. A jacaranda tree in full bloom. The real tree was just outside the attic window.

"You really captured it."

"I think it needs something more." Brick moved closer. "So do I."

"Yeah?"

"Yeah, something to make the picture right."

"Or complete."

"Are you a mind reader as well as an actor?"

"Sometimes."

Brick touched him.

"Like when I'm looking into the big brown eyes of someone simpatico."

The two men kissed, soft and then sloppy.

Brick stopped for a moment. Ray could tell something had been on his mind. "Ray, this is all pretty new to me. I just don't want to let you down."

Ray smiled. "I don't think that's going to happen. I don't think it's possible."

Their light caresses resumed where they had left off and soon became rougher. Pelvis's grinding. "You've been what's missing," managed Ray.

He wasn't sure if Brick answered, but his hands were all the response Ray needed. Each man felt the other's desire. This hunger was about more than a man satisfying a need, this hunger was about a man discovering something purer, more essential. This was about destiny. Transcendence. Completion. Ray had been with men before, but this was all new. He had no idea he could feel this way.

Brick kissed the hollow of Ray's throat and slapped him hard on the behind. Brick may have been inexperienced, but green or not that boy was catching on quick. Ray loved being handled roughly.

"Give it to me," Brick managed, fumbling with the buttons on Ray's trousers. Brick spit on his fingers and reached inside. Stroking him. The throb of excitement. A moist thrill. Cock and heart and head all beating as one, combining to become something bigger than all three.

Brick whispered, "Like that, huh? Like having me tug on it this way?" He reached around with his other hand and kneaded Ray's ass through his trousers. Not lurid. Discovering. Eager to explore and ready to please.

Brick slipped out of his pants and moved to the bed, lying back on the mattress. "Get out of those clothes."

Ray began to strip. He unbuttoned his shirt and peeled it from his striated shoulders, exposing the rise of his biceps, the curve of his chest, the hollow between his pectorals.Ray began to slide his pants down until the trousers pooled around his ankles.

"I like how your muscles move." Brick's manhood throbbed against his belly. "I like it alot." With eyes focussed on Ray, Brick lifted his penis, and let it slap back on his belly. Rigid. He put one hand behind his head and gave himself a few strong strokes with the other. His smile said that he was liking what he saw.

Ray began working his boxers. The lip of fabric moved teasingly over his ass. A glimpse. A peek. A bit more. The curve of his buttocks. The shadowy crack. Fanned hair across muscled globes. More.

Ray liked the effect his dance was having, on Brick as well as himself. He turned to the side. A glimpse from one angle. Then the other. Finally, he peeled his boxers off and tossed them to Brick. The cowboy grabbed them off his thigh and took a whiff before wrapping the shorts around his penis. Brick slapped a spot beside him on the bed. "Get over here."

When Ray approached, Brick reached up and pulled him onto the mattress. He growled into the side of Ray's neck. He ground his crotch into Ray's thigh. A breeze came through the window above them, carrying a sweet citrus scent. Brick kissed down Ray's stomach. One. Another. A third. "Such beautiful brown skin." Another kiss and Brick encountered the glans. Pulsing. When Brick licked Ray's cock leapt towards his mouth. Brick shied away momentarily. He kissed the hollows of Ray's thighs. Licked. Closer. Retreating and nearing again. The tease was driving Ray insane.

Ray grabbed the base of his penis. "Suck me."

Brick grinned and instead licked his balls. Lower. He ran a tongue across Ray's hole. Ray shifted. He wasn't ready.

Brick got on his knees and moved to the head of the bed. "Your turn." Ray was more than ready for this. His lips wrapped around Brick's erection as his hands roamed up, reaching for the cowboy's nipples. In two seconds Ray discovered that Brick liked having them tugged. Ray loved the way Brick looked when he was losing control in those moments when desire was at the wheel. Ray's tongue dipped to his balls. Lower. A tongue across his hole. Lingering. He let his tongue remain still a moment before moving ever so slightly. He parted the muscled globes as his tongue went deeper. A shiver ran through Brick's body. Not quite inside. Brick resisted. Ray wrapped a hand around Brick's waist, pulling him closer as his tongue pressed harder. Wiggling just inside. Ray pulled him more firmly onto his tongue. Brick began to relax. Then moaned. *Bingo*. Ray moved a finger there. The cowboy was trying to fight the feeling and resist the sensation. Squirming at Ray's touch, Eventually he broke away. "That... no."

Ray smiled. A clear drop of desire landed on Ray's chin. He worked his way back up. Brick was leaking like a faucet.

"You ever corn-holed a guy?" Ray finally asked with his lips still on Brick's abdomen.

Brick shook his head. "I just did what we did last night and today, but no more."

Ray smiled. "I have a real treat in store for you. Lie back." Ray sat on Brick's face. "Just close your eyes and pretend that we're kissing." Brick did as he was told. He caught on mighty quick. "You need to loosen me up a bit." Ray spread his cheeks and rocked deeper across Brick's lips and tongue. "Let your tongue explore." Brick was hesitant at first. This was nothing he ever imagined himself doing. Once he got over the thought of what he was doing, he began to enjoy himself. "That's it," said Ray. Once he had a taste, Brick grew more aggressive. Eager. When he figured he was ready, Ray got off him and used some spit to loosen himself up some more. Taking someone Brick's size might be a challenge, but Ray wanted him so badly. Desperately. He grabbed hold of Brick's manhood and began to ease it inside. Pastor Adams always said the best things in life were worth working for, though this was probably not what he had in mind. Ray closed his eyes and eased down. Wincing. Pausing. He needed to take it slow, but he was hellbent on taking every inch. "How does that feel," he asked Brick.

Brick had his eyes closed. He was already reduced to moans.

"Like that, huh? Well, you just wait." Ray began to rock his hips. Slowly, then gradually increasing speed. Brick tightened his grip on the bedding. His hands moved onto Ray's hips. Steadying. Guiding. Trying to control Ray's movements. Ray pushed his hands away. The kid from Iowa was calling the shots this time. "Come on. Tell me how good this feels."

"Incredible," was all Brick could manage.

Ray could feel Brick's excitement building. His shortened breaths and sporadic moans said it all. Ray was close behind. Ray began to stroke himself. Rocking. Clenching. Tightening and rising slow. Faster. Rocking. Riding. Faster.

"Give it to me," he said. Brick was so big. Filling him. Hitting all the right places. Again and again and again. Ray couldn't hold out. That pressure. A friction so right. Ready. "Right there."

Brick lifted his hips from the mattress. He reddened. Contorted. Ray felt the blast. The pulsing. He ran his palms across Brick's chest, grinding the heel of his hands on his nipples. Ray ejaculated a moment later and collapsed beside Brick. They held one another. The world and everything else crumbled away, leaving only the two of them. Last night had not been a fluke. Today had proven that. This moment was evidence. Both thought the other one was filthy. And both men considered that a mighty good thing.

"Why don't you move in here?" said Brick after a moment.

Ray was still catching his breath. He had been hoping Brick would say something like that but was too afraid to wish for it. Too afraid that this was all some sort of delicious delusion. Ray was already used to guarding himself against disappointment. He didn't want to be undone by expectations. "Will your landlady care?"

Brick looked into Ray's blue eyes for a moment before kissing him. "All I care about is you. I'll do what I need to do to make it right with her."

"Are you sure you wouldn't mind? You don't have to do this."

"I want to do this. I want to do it a lot." Brick kissed him again, and then again, and then again, saying yes every time. "I've never been more sure about anything."

"And you won't have regrets."

"Nope."

"And what about this…" Ray added, grabbing Brick's member.

"What about it?"

"What if I want to do this every day too, every morning when I get up and every day after work."

"You don't have to ask me twice."

Ray could imagine that sort of carrying on quite easily. He could never imagine not feeling that way about Brick..They both had a lot to learn about all this stuff, and a great partner to learn it with. Ray was ecstatic. This would have never happened in Iowa. This sort of thing only happened in fairy tales, yet it was happening to him in Hollywood. Life was so different here, so full of newness and opportunity. Ray was certain success in the movies would soon come to him as well. How could it not? He felt invincible. He was in love and everything was possible. Even better, everything seemed inevitable. The word destiny came to mind again.

Ray had a spring in his step as the two men walked back to his boarding house to settle his account and collect his belongings. They were back at Brick's attic flat just as the sun was setting in a brilliant play of orange and pink. The scent of eucalyptus was on the breeze. The all of it made it seem like the beginning of forever.

4

Brick came home from work the following Monday with a cluster of daisies in his fist. He held the bouquet behind his back. When Ray kissed him, he presented the flowers. Brick was amazed such a simple gesture could give him such purpose and make him feel so good. All his fatigue from the day disappeared, replaced with desire.

Ray blushed. "Where did you get them?"

Brick looked at his feet and confessed that he'd taken them from someone's yard. He rubbed a hand over the day's grit along the back of his neck. "People owning flowers is something I just can't get used to."

"So you took them?"

Brick nodded. "I suppose I did. The old man who lived there came out yelling bloody murder."

Ray kissed him. "You've won me. You don't have to woo me." Ray wondered if he was telling the truth as soon as he said it. Could happiness really be this easy? Could something this perfect last? Was this genuinely love or did the romantic and the actor in him create it all?

"I just want you to know I appreciate you."

Ray reached down. His desire was as strong as ever. Brick's bulge was on the verge of being obscene. "This tells me all I need to know, and this basket of yours is very eloquent."

Brick smiled. "I'm all grimy from work."

"I got just the thing," whispered Ray, reaching around to unbutton Brick's rank work shirt. He kissed the cowboy's broad back. Ray lifted one of Brick's arms and took a whiff. The smell of a working man. His working man. He gave the pit a savoring lick. Tangy. Everything about this man drove him wild. He reached around to unbuckle Brick's belt. Dug his hand inside. Reaching for that glorious thing. Turgid. That level of desire, of need, had to be almost painful. Ray undid the buttons and worked the dungarees down Brick's muscular thighs. Legs white. A stark contrast to the coppery sunburn above his waist.

Ray dropped to his knees, eager to serve his man. Brick said he could serve him in other ways. "I've got myself a list up here," Brick said, pointing to his head. Ray joked that he had created a monster.

"You're right about that. Now bend over the dresser. I need something quick." Brick positioned him and eased inside. Thirty minutes later, both men lay sweating and spent on the mattress.

After a moment, Brick kissed Ray, "You're just the thing my life was missing."

"Like in your painting."

Brick kissed him again. "Speaking of which. I want to capture you just like this."

"After what we just did? I'm all sweaty."

"You're perfect."

Ray made a hollow protest. Pastor Adams would have thought being enthusiastic about sitting for a portrait was vain. Ray smiled. Vanity is an actor's best friend. Besides, the pastor's opinions really weren't pertinent any longer. The pastor would have probably thought a lot worse about Ray's being willingly taken by another man.

Brick asked Ray to sit naked in the over-stuffed chair with one leg draped over the arm rest. "I want to capture you just as you are. I never want to forget the way I feel at this moment."

5

Ray began getting day work as an extra at the studios, then once he developed a reputation for reliability, directors gave him small featured roles. He photographed quite well. The camera not only captured his beauty, but somehow enhanced it. Ray had a small role in a western called *Kansas Outlaw*. The director gave him a close-up and told Ray he was to register desire as his leading lady walked by. After the shoot, the director gave a thumbs up to the cameraman. They knew potential when they saw it.

Visiting the set that day was a short, energetic man with a headful of red curls. He knew potential as well. He represented the film's leading lady, Barbara Lamarr. Brochman approached Ray and handed him a business card accompanied by a vigorous handshake.

Gilbert Brochman, Theatrical and Film Agent.

"You're an agent?" said Ray.

"That I am. And you need an agent, kid. You've got the raw stuff it takes to make it in this business, but that's only half of the game. You also need to have the connections. You need representation, introductions, someone to advise you, and to open doors..That someone is none other than me, Gilbert Brochman."

Ray may have been naive, but he still suspected Brochman had given that speech more than a few times. Regardless, he had heard having an agent was becoming a necessity to making it in the movies, especially for newcomers. "How does that work?"

Brochman took a seat on a crate beside Ray. "You sign the papers, and I get you work for fifteen percent of what you're paid."

"That seems little steep."

"That's because you're making so little without representation. Look at it this way. I don't make a penny if I don't get you work. If you win, I win and with me in your corner I can guarantee that you'll win. I also represent the leading lady on this picture, Barbara Lamarr, as well as Crane McCoy, Francis X. Bushman, and Fifi D'Orsay to name a few."

"Wow. And you think I have what they have?"

"I don't think, I know. It's raw, but the vitality is there. I wouldn't be wasting my time if I didn't see it. One thing about me, I will always give it to you straight. Getting to the top won't be easy, and it doesn't come without sacrifice. But if you want to get there, I promise you we can make it. You want to make it big don't you?"

Ray assured him that he did.

"That's good because you've got to be hungry for it, feel it like a burning in your belly. So what do you think? Do we have a deal?"

Ray offered a big smile. "I guess we do. Wait until I tell Brick."

"Is Brick family?"

"My... friend." Ray blushed. "My close friend."

Gilbert eyed him slowly. He seemed mighty good at reading between the lines. "You realize that's not exactly jake, right?"

"What do you mean?" Ray gave him a blank stare.

"Not good. Rotten bananas. That sort of three-letter-friend will get in your way, trip you up."

"Brick wouldn't do that."

"Don't play me for a fool. This Brick person has to go. He's a roadblock in you getting any farther. He's the sort of secret that ends careers, that stops them cold. I've seen it happen plenty of times. People have certain thoughts and expectations about film stars. There's certain things they need to be, especially if they are going to be leading men."

"You really think I could be a leading man?"

Brochman nodded. "A regular cake-eater. Look at my track record in this town. Remember, I give it to you straight. That's why I am saying you need to drop this Brick person like a hot potato. Pronto. Make it a clean break. No two ways about it."

"Maybe if I…"

"No maybes. Let's go have a bite to eat, and we can talk about it more."

Brochman made good sense. Ray knew he would have to make sacrifices if he wanted to be famous movie star. He'd expected that. He just wished Brick wasn't one of the things he needed to give up. He wondered why he had to give up one destiny to follow another. The more he listened to Brochman, the more sense he made. He wanted Brick, but he couldn't let himself get sidetracked by the first distraction that came along. He needed to show everyone in Reeversville that he was somebody. He needed to wipe their faces in it. That obligation was bigger than what he had with Brick. That would make everything worth it. He needed to prove those townsfolk wrong and vindicate his parents. For that, he was willing to make sacrifices.

Brochman gave Ray a synopsis of his career plan for him and fished a contract from the inside pocket of his suit coat. He unfolded the papers before Ray. Ray was too excited to read it through. Handing him a fountain pen, Brochman assured him it was the typical agreement between talent and agent. After only a moment's hesitation, Ray signed on the dotted line. Brochman blew on the ink to dry it. Brochman said from now on he would be known as Raymond Richmond. Ray liked the sound of that.

An hour later, Brochman said he had something already lined up for him the day after tomorrow. A strong supporting role in a studio production. "It's an Alice Terry picture. You've heard of Alice Terry, right?"

"Well sure."

"Well, this role looks like a good fit for you and the director owes me one."

By the end of the day, Brochman had Ray convinced the only way he was going to make it in the movies was to cultivate a certain image with the public. *Dashing. Youthful. Romantic. Willing to risk everything for his beloved.* "That's who your fans need to believe you to be. Fans out there don't want you to act. They want you to be the sort of characters that you play." Brochman reiterated that there was no room for Brick in that scenario. None.

"Things are happening so fast."

"That's the way opportunity happens in this town, it barges in like a drunk to a speakeasy. You have to be ready for it."

"I suppose so."

"You need to know so. Remember, we have a contract."

"But I live with Brick."

Brochman suggested a move that night. He owned a building near the studios. "You can live there for the time being. I'll just deduct the rent from your earnings."

Brochman seemed to have all the answers. Ray liked that. What he didn't like was the inevitable snag in all this stardust talk. How the hell was he going to tell Brick? If someone had told him at the start of the day about what he would be doing he never would have believed them.

Brochman gave him a ride home. "Just be straightforward," was his advice. "He's not going to want to stand in your way, not if he really loves you."

"I suppose."

"If he really loves you he'll want you to follow your dream."

"You're right."

"I'll wait right here for you to collect your things. Be quick about it."

Brick had brought dinner home from the deli on the corner. There were flowers on the table. "I paid for them this time," he said as Ray came through the door. "Rough day?"

Ray started to cry, but stopped himself. He had to remain strong. He could do this. He needed to do this if he was going to be a star. "I can't do this."

"Do what?"

"This," Ray motioned to the attic apartment.

"What?"

"I need to move out and plan more for my career. I can't have a career in movies and this too. There are sacrifices. Sometimes you can't have it all." Everything had sounded so much better when Brochman had said it. "I have a chance to have a career in the movies, but I can't be this way. Not so open. Not with men. Not with you." Ray couldn't look at Brick. Not those brown eyes. He knew if he looked into them he would see Brick's heart breaking. "I just need to collect my things." Ray tossed things in his suitcase and Brick stood to the side with his hands in his pockets.

When Ray finished packing, he kissed Brick on the cheek. Brick clenched his hands into tight white-knuckled fists. The door closed. There was silence. Deadening. Brick felt his body begin to tremble. He wondered if that had really just happened. He heard Ray descending the stairs.

Over.

It had happened. Final. Brick threw the vase of flowers across the room. He turned to the painting by the window. The canvas of Ray reclined nude before the purple flowers. Brick's face reddened. The veins in his neck stood out like cables. Anger was consuming him. Idiot. Moron. Oaf. He was all the things his Pa had always said he was. How could he have been so stupid, so gullible? Brick put a fist through the canvas and then began smashing the easel to bits. When he was finished he sat on the bed and held his head in his hands. He should have known. He should have known.

6

Brochman followed through on his promise for showier roles, and Raymond Richmond soon began attracting attention on screen as well as off. The following week, Brochman got him roles in *Riders of the Sage* and *The Bandits of Falstaff*. Brochman even finagled a couple close-ups for Ray in the latter film. Brochman convinced the executives they had something special on their hands, a real diamond in the rough. The executives agreed Brochman had done it again. Raymond Richmond began seeing his name in the gossip columns. He was referred to as an "up and coming actor," and his name was already being linked with that of several leading ladies.

At the end of the month Gage Wellmann, the head of Arcadia Films, called Ray and Brochman into the studio. "We think you're wasting your potential in these sagebrush pictures. Women seem to respond to you. I'd like to steer your career in a different direction."

Brochman said that was what he had envisioned all along. "I knew you were a smart man, Gage."

They all shared cigars to initiate this new phase of Raymond's career.

Raymond attempted to blow another smoke ring. He was getting better. He looked around Wellmann's opulent office. So this was the next step up the ladder. Cigars with the studio chief. Now he had a bona fide career and a studio behind him. "I'll do whatever you ask, Mr. Wellmann. I trust your judgement."

"Good, because next week I want to star you in *Her New Lover* opposite Bebe Daniels. I'm having the legal staffers draw up a contract now. That will be the first picture of the deal. Five pictures in the next six months."

"I'll need to review that," added Brochman

"Certainly."

Raymond tried to stop his knees from knocking. Everything was happening just as he'd planned, just as he'd hoped it would. Except for Brick. That had been regrettable. He still thought about him every night, but he assumed that would pass in time. After a couple cocktails, the memory of their lovemaking faded all together. The mess with Brick was Raymond's only regret, but it was necessary if Raymond was going to be who he wanted to be. Sacrifice was par for the course, part of the game. Dreams don't just happen.

Her New Lover was a solid box office hit that even the critics noticed. Raymond's next picture, *Calling All Flappers,* was an even bigger success. He started getting recognized and hounded for autographs. He was labelled a real sheik. The bee's knees. A four-alarm sort of fella. His face and form made women swoon. Studio publicists claimed his closeups could cause the vapors. They had a doctor and two nurses at the premiere of his next picture, *Hallelujah!,* to tend to the fainting females. Several women collapsed, photogenically swooning as he walked into the theater. It was all a publicity stunt of course, but a very effective one. The headline read *New Movie Casanova Boosts Smelling Salt Sales*. Prior to release, the title of Ray's next picture was changed from *Rose and Robert* to *Robert and Rose*. The same week Raymond Richmond was given a larger dressing room and a substantial raise.

7

After Ray walked out on him, Brick got along as best he could. That wasn't to say he was doing fine. He was feeling downright crummy. He felt betrayed. Used. Angry. Very angry. He'd always been fairly even tempered, but Brick had become more of a hot head since the breakup. He lost his temper. He got in fights, threw down his tools, and walked off more than one construction job. Coworkers figured it was woman trouble. They tried to fix him up on dates. The towering cowboy made lots of female hearts go pitter pat. Brick went out a few times and tried everything he could to take his mind off Ray.

He asked one of his dates to the movies to see *Hallelujah!* He didn't know it was a Raymond Richmond picture. He only knew that somebody at work had said it was a good date movie. When Brick saw Ray come on the screen, he felt his heart break all over again. *That asshole!* He went to the men's room and locked himself in a stall for a good fifteen minutes. When he returned, he told his date he wasn't feeling well.

"Can I get you anything?" Women were always trying to mother him. He figured the moodiness brought that out. Brick didn't need mothering, he just needed Ray.

Brick told her he had to go home. She said she would call him in the morning. Brick said that wouldn't be necessary. As he climbed the steps to his attic apartment, Brick thought about the way Ray looked up on the silver screen.

Larger than life. A god. He recalled what he looked like on this very bed, what he looked liked posing naked, or when he was on his knees pleasuring him. No less divine. Maybe even more so.

And yet, when Brick recalled that ideal man, he realized he had loved Ray's imperfections most of all. The way Ray snorted in his sleep and his tendency to grow hair on his ears and how his lazy eye took to wandering when he got tired or bored. Or the way he let out a little yelp whenever he was surprised. Those were the things that made Brick smile. The rest of it just got his dick hard. Like now.

Brick swore time and again he was done with Ray, but his heart and his body thought differently. A moment later he wrapped a hand around himself. He was already leaking a bit. He'd been half hard since he saw Ray on the screen. Tears and hormones made for an odd combination. Brick lay back on the bed and imagined Ray on top of him… No. Brick imagined Ray licking up his body starting at his toes. No. He imagined Ray simply lying there holding his hand. That was all he needed. The fantasy was simply being with him.

This wasn't the first time Brick had pleasured himself with the memory of the man who betrayed him. Every time he called himself a sap, a primo patsy. He hated himself for it. Each time he wiped that sticky hand Brick swore it was the last time. They'd only been together a couple of weeks. *Two weeks*. Not even. *Twelve Days*, Folks moved on all the time. *Like changing socks*. People who had been together months, years, decades. Why couldn't he? The thought made him feel pathetic. *And angry*. Every time he thought of Ray walking out he inevitably recalled the good stuff: the taste of Ray's ass, the contours, the tightness, the feeling of being inside him.

Brick recalled how the blue of Ray's eyes contrasted with the black of his hair. And the black tuft of hair in the hollow just above his behind. The feel of that ass when he slapped it. The way Ray sucked. Taking him all the way and fluttering his tongue along the length as he withdrew.

Before he knew it, Brick was breaking the promise to himself again. Soon he was stroking himself, faster. Imagining. Remembering. That mouth. That ass. So tight.

Brick quivered as he thought about Ray ejaculating onto his stomach while Brick used him. The tight feel of his ass clamped on Brick's erection. Tighter upon release. Silky waves. Brick reached up and tugged on his nipples. His moan reverberated in the empty attic. Empty. He was getting so close. He tightened his legs and pointed his toes. Damn him. Damn Ray for throwing everything they had away. Here it was. Brick felt the first pulse land on his chest. "Ray," he whispered. "Ray." A few moments later, Brick drifted off to sleep.

Brick stopped dating after that. If people got too nosy, he said he was a widower. *She and the baby both died in childbirth.* That quieted them down awful quick. Instead of looking for a new boyfriend or someone to replace Ray, Brick hired hustlers now and again to take care of his needs. That was easy. No confusion. No entanglements. No strings. No emotions. Just business. The commerce of pleasure. Sex for Brick became a simple transaction. The solution seemed to work for him.

Eventually independent construction work started to become a bit more scarce. The building boom had flatlined a bit. By then, Brick had gotten his temper under control. By then the wound from Ray had turned into a nasty scar. A buddy recommended that he put his name in at the studio, but he'd grown leery of depending on anyone or anything. Brick saw trust as a sucker's game. "I like being my own boss."

"That's all fine and good, but working for a studio is a steady paycheck. They're always looking for skilled builders at Metropolitan."

In the end, job security outweighed Brick's resistance. He was hired the same day he applied. He started to work round the clock at Metropolitan. Overtime. Extra hours. Some nights he even slept at the studio. There was always work to be done, sets to be built or broken down. Brick liked working. Work kept his mind off things and nothing gave him greater satisfaction than saving his money. The more his savings increased, the more secure he felt. Stable. Immune to anything that might happen. Brick vowed to make sure he was never dependent on anyone ever again.

8

After the premiere of *Robert and Rose*, Raymond had gone to a party and then another party and, as a result of the celebrations, drank far too much for his own good. Afterwards, he and a companion decided to drive down to Santa Barbara because the ocean was so lovely along the coast at night. En route, Raymond was pulled over. A highway patrolman reported that someone witnessed "unnatural carnal doings" in the vehicle at a stoplight in town. Apparently, Raymond's male companion in the auto was performing oral sex on the star. Initially Raymond was outraged that he was stopped. Eventually he offered sex to the young officer to avoid arrest. He was taken to the local jail. The studio squelched the incident and erased it completely from the police blotter. The officer in question was given a significant "tip", and the debacle was never reported. The next week, Arcadia Pictures made a substantial donation to the local police force. That was just the way things were done.

Raymond Richmond was a top ten box office star and worth the bother. Writer Elinor Glyn had just called Clara Bow The 'It Girl and when the novelist/screenwriter was asked to name Hollywood's "It' Boy she said, "There are two. Either Gary Cooper or that delightful Raymond Richmond."

That spring Raymond filmed three films back to back, oftentimes with overlapping shooting schedules. When he read the script for his next project, he tossed it into the garbage. "I am above this sort of fluff," he fumed. He was hung over and overworked and coming down from some pick-me-up powder. His nerves were frayed. Raymond not only refused to make the picture, but he demanded script approval for the final picture in his contract. Wellmann was livid.

Brochman tried to reason with him, but Raymond stayed at home and cracked open another bottle. *He was an artist! He deserved better treatment than this. He knew it, and so did his fans.*

Ray said he would listen to their offer when they were ready to talk seriously and treat him like a star rather than just an employee. "I have a reputation."

There was no debating that statement.

Wellmann threatened him with legal action. Raymond dared him. The fans clamored for their matinee idol and began a letter writing campaign against the studio. Some threatened to boycott Arcadia Pictures all together. Eventually Raymond got his way. He chose *Stranded Souls* as his next movie. The three-hankie drama was meant to showcase his dramatic range but instead showcased his dramatic limitations. The film was a modest success, but receipts were nowhere near what they had been for his lighter fare.

When Wellmann said "I told you so," Raymond reddened and accused Arcadia of sabotaging the picture to teach him a lesson. Wellmann was nonplussed at the complaint and accused Raymond of insubordination. Raymond said he didn't need him or Arcadia.

Wellmann was furious. "I made you."

"And I made you money," Raymond retorted. "Lots of money. I've paid my debt to this lousy studio."

Wellmann jabbed his cigarette in Brochman's direction. "Gilbert, reason with him. Control your client. That's your job."

"I've made you both a pretty penny," Raymond seethed.

"And I have protected you as well. Or have you already forgotten the Santa Barbara incident? Your career would be over, kaput if it wasn't for me."

"A few more scripts like the ones you've been handing me, and it will be over anyway. How do you expect me to make tripe like this work? Actors can perform magic, but not miracles."

Wellmann reddened but remained silent.

"As for the Santa Barbara incident, you were simply protecting your investment." Raymond balled his hands into fists. He looked ready to start throwing punches.

Wellmann said he'd had enough of this. He pressed a button on his desk and two baby grands in ill-fitting suits came in and stood on either side of the door. They looked like thugs from Central Casting. "Brochman, kindly take this moderately talented has been you represent out of my office before I have that poof thrown out on his perfumed butt." He pointed to the door. Raymond turned without saying another word. Both men had their pride.

Brochman complied. Once they were outside the office and heading towards their cars, Brochman explained to Raymond that he couldn't afford to make an enemy of Wellmann. Brochman said he had other clients at Arcadia. His speech was all a long blown preface to the punchline. "The time has come for us to part ways."

Ray turned to him. "Ah, go chase yourself. I'm only sorry that you beat me to it. I was about five seconds away from firing you. I need an agent who is going to represent my best interests and not his own. I need someone to do more than ride on my coattails and collect his cut."

Brochman ignored the personal attack. "I wish you the best Raymond, but you were wrong in there. Dead wrong. You shouldn't have done that."

"Are you still here? Is someone still talking? Take a hike, parasite, don't take any wooden nickels." Raymond turned and waved goodbye over his shoulder.

Word that Raymond had left Arcadia spread like wildfire. A direct confrontation with Wellmann was a juicy slice of gossip, but not the sort that ever made the tabloids. Both men had images to protect. The blow-up in Wellmann's office had been overheard by two ingenues and a screenwriter waiting in the outer office. News of the blow-out traveled by word of mouth through fitting rooms and across backlots and over cocktails at lunch. Eventually punches, a black eye, and a bloody nose were added to the story. In Hollywood even the truth was bigger.

On the way home, Raymond stopped at a roadside tavern and had a couple drinks. He always liked this place. There was a polar bear behind the bar. The owner of the speakeasy welcomed him with a smile. He had a tab there. Raymond sidled up to the bar beside a strapping young man named Tyrone who couldn't believe he was sitting right next to Raymond Richmond. "The folks at home will never believe I met you."

Raymond moved his foot a bit closer. Their shoes touched. "You remind me of myself at your age." That wasn't entire true, but Raymond was feeling horny, not honest. In the dim light, the muscular young man reminded him of Brick. After the right number of drinks, they all did.

"Really?" Tyrone's eyes grew wide. "I really would love to get into pictures."

Of course he would. They all do. And they all wanted Raymond Richmond to hold the door open and usher them inside. "To make it you have to be willing to do whatever it takes."

Tyrone agreed.

Raymond said the booze was cheaper at his place. He pushed his foot against Tyrone's shoe a bit more aggressively. "So are you willing?"

Tyrone smiled. Maybe he wasn't as naive as he seemed.

Raymond winked his way. Tyrone had taken the bait .
This was one of the perks of stardom they didn't write
about in *Photoplay*. A star can have anyone they want.
Almost anyone. Yet hook-ups of this sort always left
Raymond feeling incomplete and wanting more. None of
them were Brick.

Hours later, Raymond nudged Tyrone awake. He said he
had an early shoot.

After untangling himself from the satin monogrammed
sheets, the young man scribbled his name and phone
number on the beside pad. He left Raymond's home a few
minutes later. "Tyrone Kane. It's a rooming house, so be
sure to ask for Tyrone Kane," he had said.

Raymond nodded and kissed him goodbye. "The limo will
be here in a few, so you have to leave quickly. Best take
the side entrance. And don't talk to any of the help.
They're paid good money to keep quiet, but they talk
enough as it is."

"Sure. This will be our secret."

Our secret. Raymond had heard that before. As the young
man walked down the garden path, Raymond crumpled
the paper with his name and number and tossed it in the
waste bin. "That bugger got what he wanted."

Over breakfast, Raymond smiled to see he had received
telegrams with offers from four different studios. He was
expecting that sort of response. Wellmann was a fool. Of
course after hearing he had walked out of Arcadia, the
other film companies would scramble to sign him. One

studio promised Raymond more money, one promised greater artistic freedom, and one promised top production values. The fourth offer from Metropolitan Pictures promised all three.

Two days later, when Raymond met with J.B., the head of the Metropolitan Pictures, he smiled at the salary with options and script approval addendum and asked, "Where do I sign?" J.B. asked if he was still represented by Brochman.

"I gave him the heave ho a few days ago. I'm representing myself."

"Wise choice. Negotiate for yourself and keep your full percentage." They popped a bottle of champagne, and J.B. raised his glass. They toasted to a wonderful partnership. Raymond's first picture, *Scattered Blossoms*, a period romance with Mae Murray, was to begin shooting on Monday. "Provided you approve of the script, of course."

"So soon?"

"We're very eager to work with you. And we've had this project in place for weeks just waiting for the right leading man."

Raymond was eager to begin work on the picture as well. He waived script approval on *Scattered Blossoms*, opting to begin work on the production right away. No use causing problems at Metropolitan right out of the gate.

The studio doctor prescribed opiates to settle Raymond's nerves. "This will help you relax and give a more natural performance." When the opiates made him sluggish after long hours of shooting, he was offered amphetamines to give his performance "pep" and to keep him working eighteen hour days. Raymond took the pills frequently and without qualms. They were prescribed by a doctor, so he didn't question it. The pills helped him function and Raymond was willing to do whatever it took. *You have to make sacrifices. Like with Brick.*

Things at Metropolitan started off quite well. *Scattered Blossoms* did solid business and his follow-up, *Happy at Last,* was a smash. His next picture, *A Most Royal Scandal*, was a set back, barely breaking even at the box office. Metropolitan began having to cover up more of his indiscretions. The pills and booze made Raymond a bit more careless, but none of it really mattered. He was a star. Such things were excused and swept under the rug. Public intoxication, driving under the influence, indecent exposure, all nothing more than mishaps. And so understandable too. He was a reckless star blowing off steam. Nothing more than the vim and vigor of youth. There were no repercussions. That was part and parcel for taking care of the talent. Though Raymond was still a star worthy of having his name on the marquee, his popularity was beginning to dip. The public could be terribly fickle. Raymond blamed the directors and the scripts and Metropolitan. He hired a new manager and a new publicist in addition to his publicist at Metropolitan.

That year, *Photoplay* reported that on the matinee idol's birthday, he needed a special postal delivery for his bumper crop of fan mail. That was the publicist's story. The movie rags also reported on his love of hunting, his ermine pillow cases, his love of Egyptian art, and an entirely fictional tale of working his way to Hollywood as an amateur fighter. All Hogwash! Little of what they reported about Raymond Richmond was true. But this was Tinseltown. The truth didn't matter. In Hollywood the image was bigger than reality.

"Let's see what they've made up about me today," was a favorite phrase of his as he opened any of the plethora of movie magazines he liked to peruse during breaks in filming. There were dozens of tabloids. *Grist for the mill* is the phrase many of the seasoned Hollywood veterans used to describe them. A new motion picture magazine seemed to hit the stands every week.

9.

Raymond arrived early the first day on the set of his next picture, *Eastern Adventure*. After the lukewarm response to *A Most Royal Scandal*, he was anxious to begin work on a new project and was hopped up on amphetamines. Jazzed. Revved. He tried to review the pages of script scheduled for shooting, but he had trouble retaining some of the words. He found it difficult to concentrate with all that pounding. They were still building a wooden bridge that was to be the lover's rendezvous spot in the first scene. "A secret rendezvous in the middle of a bridge?" Raymond laughed. "Not terribly discreet. Only in Hollywood."

The pounding continued. Raymond was on the verge of calling the director to demand that construction cease or be continued off site when he saw the source of the disturbance. One of the crew with a hammer. Brick. *Brick?* He'd know that long torso, the muscled back, that backside, those strong arms, and that squared head anywhere. *Brick.* Here. Raymond felt the tingling in his stomach. The sight took his breath away. He wondered if Brick had seen him?

Raymond eased himself from his chair and went back to his dressing room. Brick. He remembered the attic room and those lazy days and endless nights of love making. Such pure desire. Satisfaction complete and beyond compare. Better than any drug or lover or thrill he had found since. Maybe even better than success. They had been mad for one another. Life seemed so much simpler then, before his career. *Before all this*. Raymond was jarred from his reverie by a knock on his trailer door.

"Mr. Richmond, you're wanted on set."

When Raymond returned to the set, the bridge was completed and none of the construction crew remained in sight.

Had that really happened? Sometimes he worried that too many pills were making him see things. Not this time. He was sure that had been Brick.

Raymond kept forgetting his lines or laughing without cause for amusement. The crew had been warned about his erratic behavior. Most thought it was the drugs. That was the rumor on the lot, but Raymond Richmond was box office and worth the retakes. Even though they were a couple days behind schedule, Richmond was the reason the picture was being made. Eventually the day's pages were shot.

Before leaving the set, Raymond called a production assistant aside. He said he needed a favor. "I need some shelves built in my dressing room. I need somewhere to store my scripts."

"Of course Mr. Richmond," said the assistant.

"I'd like them built as soon as possible."

"I'll have someone attend to it."

"There is a specific someone I want. I've heard good things about a construction crew member named Brick. He does carpentry work here. Brick the carpenter," he added with a laugh. "He was on the set earlier today. I'd like him to build and install the shelving unit."

"Oh yes, you can count on it Mr. Richmond." The production assistant made the proper notation on his clipboard. He looked up. "And I can have the shelving unit installed tomorrow when you are on set so the noise won't disturb you."

"I'd rather they be done when I am there, so I'm sure they are being done properly."

"Yes, Mr. Richmond. You can count on that tomorrow."

Tomorrow. Raymond smiled. No word had ever been filled with more promise or greater anticipation. He'd be seeing Brick tomorrow. Raymond remembered that sweet man and his glorious manhood. Maybe this was what he'd been missing in his life, what made being a star less fulfilling than he thought it would be. Maybe he only needed someone who loved him as Ray. The breakup had really been Brochman's doing. Maybe being with Brick might fill the void the hooch and drugs couldn't. Maybe things could be different between them now that Raymond was somebody. The flip side of success was that it attracted a lot of phonies. Raymond needed someone who loved him for who he was rather than what he was. He needed someone he could trust.

Raymond changed clothes a half dozen times before heading to the studio the following day. He arrived early and went straight to his dressing room. Brick was already there, taking measurements. The smell of freshly sawed wood was in the air.

"Hello, Brick."

"Hello, Mr. Richmond."

Raymond smiled. So that was how Brick was going to play the scene. "I've missed you."

Nothing.

"Did you hear me?"

No answer.

"Brick I've missed you." Raymond's arms encircled him from behind. "I've needed you so badly."

Raymond put a head on this shoulder. "I understand your being angry. I had no choice. I had to do it for my career, Brick. What if I told you it could be different now. I'm different now. I'm somebody. I'm the 'It' Boy. I was just a nobody then." Raymond turned him around. He didn't see anything in Brick's brown eyes except watery redness.

"I always thought you were something special," Brick said, "from the first time I set eyes on you at that party you were it for me."

Raymond dropped to his knees. He wanted Brick so badly. Desperately. He needed Brick to make his life better. He needed Brick to make him feel good. "Let me show you how much I've missed you, and then you can show me how much you've missed me."

Raymond offered him a bit of cocaine. Brick declined. Raymond took a snort and a moment later his hands were fumbling with Brick's belt. Rubbing. Pulling him closer. Brick tried to bat his hands away. "We'll get in trouble."

"No, we won't. No one tells me what to do. Trust me. Things are different now. It's a different world."

"For some of us."

"For both of us." Raymond began kissing the crotch of Brick's work pants. Saliva markings covered the fabric.

Despite his eagerness, Raymond unzipped Brick's pants slowly, tooth by tooth. He rubbed Brick's swelling groin with his hand., moving his mouth forward. He slipped his tongue in the fly of his boxers and licked the side of his rod. Enough with the prelude. Raymond pulled the shorts beneath Brick's scrotum. When he did Brick's erection sprang upward at a powerful angle. "More beautiful than ever," Ray said, licking up the ventral and then dorsal side before taking the head into his mouth. Brick still smelled like a man. Musky. Gritty. Virile. Basic. Like the earth. Miles away from the artifice of this place. Brick's penis hit the back of Ray's throat. Ray fluttered his tongue on the underside as he came back up its length and kept only the helmet in his mouth.

Brick let out a moan and bent his legs a bit, using his arm to steady himself against the wall. The planks for the shelving unit toppled to the floor.

Raymond smiled. He had him now. He released Brick from his mouth and stroked him a few times with the excess saliva. "Brick, I want you inside of me. I want you so bad." Raymond was already reaching back and using two fingers to loosen himself.

Brick needed no further encouragement. He pulled Raymond up by the collar and bent him over the dressing room desk. Raymond pushed the hairbrush and scripts and writing set aside. Everything clattered to the floor. *Who gives a damn?* "Do it," said Raymond.

Brick eased inside. Raymond did a quick intake of breath. *Relax. Relax.* Brick began to move slowly. Trying to be quiet, cognizant of the set noises and passing voices just outside the trailer. Business as usual beyond the thin walls. His balls gently slapped Raymond's ass cheeks, mixing with their light moans. Brick reached around and stroked Raymond. He made his fist slick with spit and returned it there, letting Raymond fuck his fist as Brick filled his ass. "You like this? You missed it?" Brick whispered in his ear. The pace quickened. Sex had become a race to the finish line.

"Oh yeah," Raymond moaned.

Brick shushed him. "Not so loud."

"Come on, Brick. Give it to me."

Raymond had been with Brick enough to know that the cowboy was getting close.

As if on cue Brick whispered in his ear, "You about there?"

"I'm with you. I'm with you." Raymond said, leaning back to kiss Brick.

Someone knocked on the door. "Five minutes, Mr. Richmond."

"Okay," he called, attempting to respond a normal voice. He began to tense. His legs shook. He was on the brink. The peak. Poised. Almost there, almost… Ahhhhhhh.

Raymond's first eruption coated Brick's hand More seed landed on the dressing room table.

Brick took a bit on his finger and brought it to his mouth. The taste was all the cowboy needed to push him over the top. His knees buckled as he felt himself begin to drain.

Brick remained inside him and held him close.

Still bend over the table, Raymond took another snort of coke. Suddenly Brick was making him claustrophobic.

Raymond pulled away. Brick buckled up and Raymond rushed into costume. Luckily, an overcoat required for the scene covered the swelling in his crotch. "Duty calls." Raymond downed a couple pills from a bottle on the dressing table and opened the trailer door. "Ready."

No one on set seemed the wiser.

The day's shoot was long and grueling. Raymond required repeated takes of his first scene. He simply could not get it right. He saw the script girl shake her head and whisper to the director for the umpteenth time. Raymond knew he'd gotten the line wrong. The director finally asked if anything was bothering him.

Raymond said he'd be fine, but he knew his performance was off. He felt it. He asked the director if they could break for lunch. "I just need a little time." By then, Brick was finished with the shelves. Gone. Over the lunch break, Raymond did a bit of nose powder and had a highball. He worried Brick was throwing off his work. Distracting him. He couldn't concentrate. Raymond concluded that having Brick there was the problem. Maybe Brochman had been right about that after all. The more Raymond thought about it, the angrier he became. Even knowing Brick was working for Metropolitan was disturbing. Who knew when he would show up on set again?

When Raymond came back from lunch, the director asked if he was okay. Raymond confessed something had been bothering him. He'd had a disturbing encounter with a worker on set. "He was building shelves in my dressing room and... " He didn't go into details but alluded to the fact that Brick might be a tabloid spy or that he might have stolen something from him. "I'm under a lot of pressure. We all are with this production. You know I'd be the last person to complain, but I'd just feel better, less anxious, if this Brick person weren't on the lot."

10.

Brick regained consciousness in the County General Hospital three days later. He ached all over. Battered. Bruised. Broken. Stitched. Looking down, he moaned to see he was bandaged from head to toe. His head throbbed. He couldn't think beyond the shroud of pain. *Where the hell was he?* Brick had no idea what had happened. He was simply here.

At the sound of his moans, the nurse appeared at his bedside. "You were in a nasty accident."

Brick's vision slowly began to adjust. Focus.

"Just breathe, slowly."

Brick did as he was told. The room was so bright, it hurt his eyes to look for too long. A dark-haired man stood before him. "Who are you?"

The man brought a glass of water to Brick's cracked lips. "I've been taking care of you. My name is Lou. I'm your nurse."

Brick tried to sit up. *Bad idea*. He winced and fell back upon the pillows.

"Not so fast," Lou said, easing him back down.

Brick took another sip of water, "How bad is it?" he finally managed.

"Well, you'll live, but not because of your driving skills. You smelled like a distillery when they brought you in here. Things were touch and go for the first twenty-four hours, but you stabilized eventually. How fast were you going anyway? The drivers who brought you in three days ago figured you should be scheduled for a funeral about now."

"What? Three days!" The outburst made him wince. Brick turned his head on the pillow. When he closed his eyes, some of the pain faded away. "And what's the damage?"

"Broken hands, bruised ribs, fractured pelvis, and a nasty little souvenir here." Lou pointed to the bandage that covered half of Brick's face.

Brick could feel the skin or the bandages there. Thread? Stitches? The wound itched.

"You shouldn't have been driving."

Brick's lips thinned. "I know."

"You could have killed someone else instead of your truck, or that tree."

"I know."

Lou shook his head. "You sure know a lot for a guy that acted so damn stupid."

"Is this lecture about finished?" Brick his head turned away and fell asleep a few moments later. Maybe his nurse had had been right. He was an idiot.

Brick slept for another twenty-four hours.

When Lou asked Brick about Ray a few days later, Brick said never mind. "Ray is just someone I used to know."

"So was this Ray the reason you wrapped your truck around that tree?"

Brick spit out the straw. "Just stick to nursing. This is none of your business." He could see the comment had hurt Lou's feelings. "I don't want to be cruel, but please. Don't pry. Just let me be."

A week later the doctor removed Brick's facial bandages. The cut from his hairline to his jaw still looked bad. "This is going to leave quite a scar," the doctor had said.

Brick didn't care. Maybe that scar would be a good reminder not to be such a damn fool. He'd see it every time he looked in the mirror and hopefully he'd remember the reason he was sporting it.

After the bandages were removed, the doctor gave the okay to start rehabilitation. Lou began working with Brick more intensely, helping him to stand and walk. His hands would take a while to heal. Lou said he might not be able to return to carpentry or to his painting.

"How do you know about my painting?"

"You talked about it when you were unconscious. You talked about all sorts of things."

The comment made Brick feel uneasy. He didn't like the thought of saying God knows what in front of a bunch of strangers. He didn't like to think about what he might have revealed. *What had he said?*

"But we won't know anything for sure regarding manual dexterity," Lou added.

Brick was beginning to smell like a pig sty. Sponge baths could only take away so much of the grime and the stink. "Today we're going to try to get you in a real tub for an honest to goodness bath. How's that sound?"

Despite the fact that they sometimes butted heads, Brick had grown to like Lou. He owed him a great deal. Lou wanted only what was best for him. That much was clear. Lou had also endured the brunt of Brick's sour attitude and still remained committed to Brick's recovery. That level of dedication was rare.

Lou helped Brick into the bathroom. He was still hobbling and yellow with bruises, but his pelvis was almost mended, and the soreness of his ribs was almost gone. He was no longer in agony every time he breathed. Brick stretched out his arms and Lou undid the ties along the back, sliding his hospital gown off his arms. Brick leaned against him, naked as Lou lowered him into the tub. "How's that?"

Brick nodded.

"Now let's get some of this stink off of you." Lou began to lather the sponge before moving it in firm broad strokes over Brick's muscled shoulders and back. "How's that feel, buddy? Keep your hands up, over your head and out of the water. I don't want to get those bandages wet."

"Feels terrific." Once Lou was done with his back and shoulders, Brick leaned back in the tub.

Lou soaped his chest. Brick's nipples hardened under the firm scratch of the sponge. He shifted a bit uncomfortably in the tub. Lou worked the sponge down farther, across Brick's hard belly, beneath the surface of the water. Brick leaned back in the water with his eyes closed. The bath and the sponge felt so good. So good. He felt himself drifting away, and then he noticed a stirring in his crotch. Daydreaming. Feeling so good. It had been so long. He sat up in the tub, embarrassed at the beginnings of his arousal. "I…"

"Just relax," said Lou, easing him back into the warmth of the water. "Just relax and let me do the work."

Lou applied more soap on the sponge and put it beneath the water on his inner thighs, moving up to soap Brick's testicles. "Keep your hands up." Brick's member began to swell and expand. The head of his cock enlarged, breaking through the soap bubbles along the water's surface. Lou gripped his penis in his hand and began to soap either side of it with the sponge. Brick leapt at his touch. "Sorry…"

"Don't be sorry. Just a normal response. Relax and keep your hands up." Brick lay back in the tub as Lou continued to soap his genitals. Reaching deep, Lou dragged the sponge over his behind and lingered to clean his asshole before moving the sponge back up to his balls, soaping the surface before returning to clean his penis. Lou moved to his arms. Brick opened his eyes and looked at him and then down. "Please, just a bit. I need it so bad and my hands…"

They both knew what he was talking about.

Lou put down the sponge and locked the bathroom door. He wrapped his hand around him. "How's that feel?"

Brick answered with a moan.

Lou wrapped his soap slick hand tighter around Brick's tool. Brick's eyes were closed and his lips were softly moving.

"Ray," Brick whispered. The moment he did, his eyes opened and his penis began to deflate.

Lou pushed him back into the tub. "You've got it bad. Close your eyes. Let me be Ray. Let me be him for today." Lou added more soap to his hand and continued. Brick's full erection returned in seconds, swelling to even greater dimensions. Brick moaned. A moment later Brick began to twitch. So close. On the brink.

"Let it go,".

Brick began to move his hands downward. Lou whispered to keep them up. Brick arched his back, bringing his cock and balls out of the soapy water. So perfect. Almost there. Lou increased the speed of his strokes. "Now. Now."

Brick's face contorted. The first squirt of semen shot over his head and hit the tile wall. Spurt after spurt followed. Lou used the come he had on his hand to bring himself to orgasm a moment later.

The moments after were awkward. Lou slipped himself back in his shorts and stood. "Now let's get you cleaned up." he said, pulling the drain out of the tub.

Brick caught his eye. He saw that the nurse was deeply conflicted over what had transpired. "It's okay. I asked for that. And I needed it, badly. I think we both did."

Lou helped him to stand in the tub and step out onto the floor. Lou began drying him, rubbing and caressing his skin with the thick cotton towel. "I just wish…"

Brick motioned for Lou to be quiet and kissed him gently on the mouth. "My head says you would be perfect for me, but my heart is saying something else. There's someone else I need to get out of my head first. That wouldn't be fair to you."

"Ray?'

"Ray."

"Well, I'm not asking for anything more, nothing really. Maybe I could help you forget him or at least try to take his place. Maybe in time."

Brick kissed Lou again. Why couldn't he have fallen for a guy like this? Someone who cared about him. Kind.

Understanding. Giving. A man with his best interests in mind. Someone who was ready for a relationship. Someone's whose life didn't seem all that complicated. "This business with Ray is something I have to do all by myself."

"This Ray must be quite a guy."

Brick exhaled through his teeth. Until the words came out of his mouth, he had no idea how he was going to answer. "Actually he is a jerk, a lowdown jerk. But I love him. After all this, that's the real kicker. He's the reason I got behind that wheel with a belly of rotgut and a death wish. Not because I hated him, but because despite everything, I still love him."

11

As the months passed, Raymond began to notice the tabloids ran fewer stories about him. At the peak of his career that would have pleased him, but not anymore. He blamed Metropolitan. "I had more coverage when I was with Arcadia," he complained. As a result, Raymond hired another publicist and then fired him and hired another when the problem was not resolved. The following month even fewer items about him appeared. Just pieces that featured fresher talent and newer faces. The entire thing made no sense to him. What the hell was going on in this town? Raymond suspected it was a conspiracy. Plenty of people had it out for him, starting with Wellmann.

There was no conspiracy. The lessening of Raymond Richmond's popularity was simply the arc that most careers follow. Raymond was no longer news, his name no longer appeared in *Favorite Star* polls. Newer stars grabbed headlines and features. His movies were no longer so widely anticipated. Despite the costly production values and salary, the box office performance of Raymond's pictures had become unreliable. And the studio rarely enjoyed surprises of that sort. Disappointing was the word that often described his movies.

Raymond's career decline coincided with the advent of sound pictures in the late 1920s. Talking pictures changed everything. Patrons found talkies novel and exciting, leaving the entire town in an upheaval. So much of what seemed to be a given only weeks before became uncertain overnight. Things in vogue only last year suddenly seemed archaic. Theater owners scrambled to adapt their movie palaces to sound and clamored to book talking pictures. The result in Hollywood was chaos. The studios rushed sound films into production. The change in the medium caused by sound even resulted in a shift in the the world's notion of romance. Stars became less distant and mysterious and, as a result, a record number of careers were launched. Even more were left in ruins.

Raymond complained to anyone who would listen and several who would not, that talking pictures were a fad, and that they would destroy the motion picture industry, undermine the mystery. He was adamant that his next picture,*Vanguard,* would be a silent one. "By then, this will have all blown over." On the set, Raymond had a make-up man fired because he was overheard raving about a talking picture. The following week he had a continuity girl suspended for similar reasons. His tirades on the set were now legend at the studio. Temperamental seemed too tame a term. As per his demands, *Vanguard* was made as a silent picture. The film was never released in the U.S.

Though everyone except Raymond knew it, talking pictures were not the primary reason for his career problems. Unprofessionalism and indiscretion, combined with the booze and the pills ended Richmond's top movie-making days at Metropolitan Pictures. The studio was paying increasing amounts of hush money to quell his scandals. With his diminishing ticket sales, covering up the salacious details of his indiscretions simply became not worth the trouble. The studios had graver concerns and didn't have the time, patience, or energy to fuss with the needs of a now second tier star. The final receipts of *Vanguard* even made his place as a second tier star somewhat shaky. Raymond Richmond was easily replaceable. J.B.'s decision not to renew Raymond's contract was met with a sigh of relief by almost everyone at Metropolitan from the hair and make-up people, to the directors, to the legal staff, to the accountants.

The last straw with the studio happened one August evening a few months after *Vanguard* had wrapped production. Raymond was caught performing an act of fellatio on a lifeguard at a public beach. Raymond knew it had been unwise, but he'd grown used to having little to no repercussions for his actions. J.B. had done an even better job than Wellington of protecting the reputation of his star. That night, Raymond had gone for a drive, and the moonlight was so lovely. He was nervous about how his latest film would be received. He had been so adamant about not doing a sound picture, and now that was all audiences seemed interested in seeing. He'd miscalculated the appeal of talkies and now there was no undoing what he had done.

Raymond brought a bottle at the beach, and he was cursing yet again the sweeping changes that were happening in Hollywood. *Why couldn't things simply remain as they were?* Silent sets were being dismantled and destroyed and sound stages were being built around the clock. Now all the contracted players were being forced to endure microphone tests. The process was frightening and degrading. The Talmadge sisters became has-beens overnight. John Gilbert ruined. Raymond shuddered. A star of his stature, having to undergo such nonsense as a talking audition. It was absurd! Demeaning. Terrifying.

And in the midst of all this, a young man had come along the beach and asked if he was okay. Before he could answer, the lifeguard had said, "Hey, you're Raymond Richmond."

Raymond looked the young man up and down. He could see the young man's muscular chest beneath the thin fabric of his shirt. "In the flesh," Raymond had said, taking a bow. His ego needed some strokes and maybe even a little something more. Raymond plopped down on the sand. "Come sit beside me."

The lifeguard did as the star requested. After all, this was Raymond Richmond.

Raymond asked his name.

"Mitch."

Raymond was slurring his words. "Mitch, I was just a nobody from Reeversville once, a lot like you I suppose."

Mitch nodded.

"And I would have done anything, anything to be in the movies."

Mitch said he'd love to be in pictures.

That was all Raymond needed to hear. "Well, how would you like to make a top box office star very, very happy?"

"Sure," the lifeguard nervously replied .

"I don't say this to just anybody. I can have my pick you know." Raymond was slurring his words. "I am only saying this because you look like the sort of tasty treat that could make me very happy." Raymond put his hand on Mitch's crotch. "I like big boys," he laughed. "Are you a big boy?"

The lifeguard blushed.

Raymond knew that the direct approach rarely failed, especially when you're a star. How could it? What mortal refused when he was being summoned by a god? Raymond lured Mitch to an outcropping of rocks and dropped to his knees. Mitch had a beautiful cock. "You are a big boy," Raymond smiled.

Mitch asked about motion pictures and the real lives of all his favorite stars almost the entire time. "Is Clara Bow really as wild as they say?" Raymond was too busy sucking to pay him much mind. Besides, he could barely hear him above the pounding surf. Visitors on the beach that night could see more than Catalina in the distance, and they notified the authorities.Raymond and the lifeguard soon found themselves in a different sort of spotlight.

Studio representatives with padded wallets arrived on the scene only moments after two bulls showed up with cuffs. The payoff was costly. The following day, J.B. summoned Raymond into his office. There were several studio executives present in the room. J.B. didn't even rise from his chair. The studio agreed to cover up the scandal, but Raymond's contract was hereby amended on the spot. He would no longer be given script or director approval on his final four pictures with Metropolitan. The remaining films would not be top productions, but would instead be talking pictures with a second tier budget contingent on the results of his sound test.

Raymond expected to be resoundingly chastised, but he wasn't expecting this. "What if I don't agree?"

J.B. was clearly enjoying this. "The terms are no longer up to you. That is simply how it is going to be."

"B pictures? Sound test?" Raymond reddened and clenched his fists. The studio execs and J.B. himself countered that this was Raymond's chance to prove he was still a top box office star. "If you're going to regain your star status, this is your opportunity. Most studios wouldn't give you a chance."

"I have nothing to prove. I am a star!" Raymond fumed, storming out of the meeting.

"Someone needs to advise that guy to take a long hard look in the mirror," said one of the executives.

J.B. shook his head. "Too bad, really. Raymond Richmond had talent, or at least charisma, at one time."

"Only four more pictures with that buffoon!" laughed another of the executives after the door slammed. The others cheered at the comment.

Leaving the studio that day, Richmond drove to a seedy part of town for more weed and cocaine before heading to another speakeasy. J.B. and his posse couldn't do this sort of thing to him. He'd made them a lot of money. *A lot of money*. Metropolitan owed him. They all owed him. When Raymond woke up the next morning, he had no memory of getting home. He remembered his third round of drinks and that was about it. He paid little attention. His blackouts had become so routine he had stopped wondering what happened. He figured if it was anything catastrophic, he'd find out about it soon enough. When he checked his coat pockets the tea and nose powder were gone.

No one placed very high hopes on any of the four remaining pictures he was contracted to make. All four features were bottom of the bill productions and practically slated to fail. J.B. had seen to that. The remaining Raymond Richmond movies were all given lackadaisical budgets, novice directors, and slashed production values. In the most successful of them, he played the villain in a detective series. Raymond's days of saving a picture with his presence had been over for a couple years. Everyone except Raymond was wise to that fact. He left Metropolitan at the end of his final shooting day with no farewell, no thank you, and little fanfare. Just a bottle under his arm and a cardboard box of things from his dressing room. The guard didn't even nod as Raymond drove his Duesenberg Model J through the front gates a final time.

In *Variety*, both parties claimed his leaving the studio was amicable decision due to creative differences, but it didn't fool many in Hollywood. Most in the movie business had heard plenty of rumors about Raymond Richmond. His leaving Metropolitan was hardly headline news anyway. It was better described as being a page five item with no details, simply the facts. The fans had spoken, or in Raymond's case, they had maintained a profound silence. The past was the past. On with the new. Much more space was being devoted to the doings of Robert Montgomery, Miriam Hopkins, Gary Cooper, and Joan Crawford's newest picture.

Raymond expected Metropolitan to have second thoughts. He found it hard to believe the studio was abandoning him after all the money he'd made for them. *Such ingratitude.* He'd dined with royalty. His footprints were in Grauman's forecourt, for goodness sakes. Being released from his contract felt like a break-up, and Raymond fed his misery with booze. Sure his pictures hadn't been making as much money recently, but that sort of thing happened now and again. Audiences could be fickle. A blizzard in the midwest, and any film's receipts could take a hit. So-so pictures and lukewarm reception were just part of the industry. They didn't mean a thing. Not really. Raymond knew the way this town worked. One strong production, and he'd be back on top. All he needed was one good picture. All he needed was someone willing to give him the chance. Then Metropolitan would be sorry. After that J.B. would be begging him to come back.

12

When Brick was released from the hospital after eight weeks, he was uncertain how he was going to support himself. The bandages on his hands had been removed, but his fingers were still swollen and sore and his ability to grasp was greatly diminished. Lou told him that capacity would return eventually. Lou said that if he was having any sort of trouble, or he just wanted company, that he could call or visit or even move in. "I have a decent sized place, and it doesn't have to mean anything," he had said.

But Brick knew it would. The weekly relief Lou had provided during his baths already meant something to the nurse. Brick was sure of it. Lou was already compromising his ethics for Brick's pleasure. He wouldn't do that if it meant nothing. Brick shook his head and ducked into the waiting taxicab, "Thanks Lou, but I need to be on my own and figure some things out." Brick didn't want to give him any false hopes. For whatever reason, the magic simply wasn't there, not like it had been with Ray.

"That's quite a battle scar you got there," said the cabbie, adjusting his hat.

Brick told him his address. "I got in a fight with a tree. The tree won. Now, I take cabs."

"Good to hear," he replied, pulling the taxi from the curb.

Given the extent of his injuries, carpentry was no longer an option for Brick. Even the manual dexterity required for painting was impossible during his early convalescence and recovery. Maybe one day. He still had his oils. He'd bought a new easel. Back in his attic apartment, Brick was soon bored out of his mind. Luckily he'd been frugal and still had a good amount of savings. Luckily he'd avoided the stock market. The crash had wiped a lot of folks out completely.

Mrs. Hanover brought him meals and did his laundry. The first time she saw his face, she dropped the meal she was carrying and crossed herself. A facial scar from scalp to jaw was a terrible shock. Brick reminded himself he needed to warn people about it in the future. He took to wearing his hat dipped low so he didn't cause any heart attacks.

The next day Mrs. Hanover came by to cut his hair. She had always cut her late husband's. She said he had a thick head of hair until the day he died. She asked Brick what he was going to do now. Brick said he wasn't sure. Mrs. Hanover assured him that things would be okay. She said she just knew they would. "God has a plan."

Brick nodded. He had to wonder what God's plan for him could possibly be.

"Where is your friend that used to stay with you?"

Brick asked her who, but he knew the friend she was talking about.

"Handsome. Dark, dark hair."

"Ray," Brick said.

"Yes."

"Ray went away."

Brick figured that Mrs. Hanover had never made the connection that Ray was Raymond Richmond, but then again Brick had never known the old woman to actually go to the movies. Mrs. Hanover shook her head, "Too bad. He made you so happy."

She finished cutting his hair in silence. Brick liked the short haircut she gave him. Combing anything longer would not be easy for a while, not with his hand injuries.

On his third night out of the hospital, Brick met with Rizzo and Cole, a couple of his buddies who still worked construction for Metropolitan. They were Italian and Irish respectively and also were brothers-in-law. "Holy shit!" they said in unison, seeing his scar.

"Now we're going to be working overtime to find you a wife," Rizzo had said. Cole agreed. Brick had never told them anything about himself and men. They were good guys, but they wouldn't understand. Fairies were the sort of people they joked about or something they called others as an insult. Being a fairy or a limp-wrist seemed about the worst thing a man could be. Brick could never tell them.

Cole slapped Brick on the back and said they brought a straw so he could keep up with the drinking. Brick laughed and said it would be the first time he ever drank a beer that way. After an hour or so of drinking and talking about their families and Brick's recovery, Cole had said, "Well, did you hear? Richmond got his."

Everyone knew Raymond was the one who got Brick fired from Metropolitan. However, no one except Raymond and Brick knew the real reason behind his dismissal from the studio. Folks just figured it was another of Raymond's tirades.

Brick asked what he meant.

"The studio cancelled Raymond Richmond's contract."

"Just like that," said Rizzo with a snap of his finger. "Gone. If you ask me, there's more to the story. Now that miserable drunk is taking whatever picture work he can get from whoever is willing to hire him."

Cole confirmed it with a tilt of his drink. "Like I say, what goes around comes around. There's no more to the story than that."

Brick said he'd drink to that, and he immediately felt conflicted. He wanted so much to be able to hate Ray, but he couldn't. He found no pleasure in toasting his misfortune.

By the time he came back to the conversation, Cole and Rizzo were going on about how talking pictures had changed just about everything at the studio. "We're building those sound sets like nobody's business."

"Fat lot of good that does me," said Brick, holding up his hands.

Cole nodded. "You'll heal."

Brick was curious about the technology of sound pictures. He had always been intrigued by the technical aspect of design. If he had remained at the studio, he probably would have moved into that field. Building seemed like somewhat of a dead end, but not technological advancement. That part of the business was constantly evolving. Brick's cronies said it was a good time to come on board at the studio.

Brick almost choked on his beer. "Not a chance. Besides, I think I am officially banned."

"Nah. We'll put in a good word," said Rizzo.

Cole took a swig of his brew. "Given all the bad blood, getting canned because of Richmond will be like a recommendation." He said the sound guys could use all the help they could get.

Brick declined but asked more about the sound problems.

Rizzo and Cole talked about the difficulty of filtering out background noise since the recording microphones seemed to pick up every nuance of sound. "The sound guys are always complaining about it." Director Dorothy Arzner had recently developed the boom microphone, which increased the ease of mobility during a scene.

"You know her. Good director, dresses like a man," added Cole.

Brick knew her.

Rizzo called for another round of drinks. "That boom thing only solved one problem, but sound is causing a lot of other problems as well."

Brick had long ago realized problems were little more than unrealized opportunities. He got that can-do attitude from his Ma. Pa always saw the wrong in things. But his Ma never let troubles get her down for long, even though they had troubles aplenty growing up in Montana.

"There goes Mr. Sunshine," Cole said with a slap on Brick's back.

Rizzo said he'd been waiting for it.

Folks used to joke and call Brick Mr. Sunshine when he looked on the bright side of things. That was after his fighting days, of course. Brick took the good natured ribbing in stride and toasted his mother. Rizzo and Cole raised their glasses in unison. Brick had missed these guys. They were good men, but Brick had to wonder if they would treat him the same way if they knew the real reason he was fired from Metropolitan. He doubted it. Folks could be that way about things they didn't understand. He might have turned out that way if he never met Ray.

After he bid the boys goodnight, Brick thought about the difficulty the studio was experiencing with sound. He couldn't shake the thought from his mind. He thought of it as a puzzle he wanted to solve. Brick wondered about developing a filter to encase the speaking device, blocking secondary noise beyond a certain distance. That night he dreamt about the sort of apparatus that might do the trick. His Ma used to say those inspired nighttime thoughts were the angels whispering. She claimed angels always come to solve problems in our sleep. The trick was teaching yourself to listen to them. His Pa had called her ideas hogwash. Mocked her. Soon she never spoke of the angels in front of his Pa, but only to Brick.

Over the next few weeks, as his hands continued to heal, Brick followed his angel whisperings and puttered with different materials and shapes until his idea was a tangible object. He constructed a carbon insulated conical recording device which was a vast improvement over the current microphones being used. Brick promptly took it to a patent lawyer, filed the proper paperwork, and had his invention registered. Two months later, he presented a prototype to the major studios. Four out of the five big film companies were enthusiastic about the demonstration model and were eager to incorporate this new technology. What's more, they were willing to pay handsomely for it.

The device made Brick a wealthy man overnight. He was kept on as a sound advisor at First National but was able to name his own hours. He didn't have to work. Brick said goodbye to Mrs. Hanover and, giving her a more than generous gift, moved out of his attic domicile. His business manager suggested he invest in property. Brick bought an apartment building across town, and then another. The Great Depression meant property was cheap. After those two buildings he purchased a bungalow with a garden in a complex off of Sunset Boulevard. Lots of no frills movie people lived there. His needs weren't fancy, but he liked to be comfortable. He liked to have some space. By then, his hands were recovered enough for him to return to painting.

Brick spent little on food and entertainment and even less on clothing. His tastes weren't extravagant, but he did purchase a new car. After buying the properties, he put most of his remaining earnings from the newfangled microphone directly into the bank. Since the advent of the Depression, banks had to guarantee a man's savings. The government made sure of that. The FDIC made Brick feel secure. The one extravagance he did indulge in was that he began hiring rent boys two or three nights a week. He had needs that could not be denied. After all, he was a thirty-year-old red-blooded and virile man. Hustlers didn't give a damn about his scar. A couple even claimed they considered it sexy.

13

For a solid week, Raymond waited for Metropolitan to ask him to return. He sat and drank and stared at the telephone. He smoked opium and waited, but J.B. never called. For the first time since firing Brochman, Raymond hired an agent. Despite Bernie's big talk, he was suspiciously silent regarding negotiations with Metropolitan. Finally Raymond told Bernie to forget Metropolitan. "Their loss," he fumed.

Raymond had bigger concerns. He had been far from frugal with his money. He needed cash. He was in hock up to his eyeballs. As soon as Bernie spread the word that Raymond Richmond was a free agent, several interested producers came forward to offer him projects. No contracts, just one time deals. The stock market crash dried up two of the offers, but Raymond did manage to find work. After all, he still had his fans though they could no longer be described as a legion. To some, Raymond Richmond was still a name, but Hollywood had the memory of a fruit fly. Perhaps after a few hit films, Raymond could make Metropolitan sorry they had ever let him go. "That would show J.B." Success would mean sweet revenge. Raymond told Bernie to send him the scripts. "Raymond Richmond is ready to go back to work."

That anticipated success never materialized. Raymond freelanced at lesser studios for almost two years. He still looked good, and when he wasn't slurring his words, his low soothing voice allowed a smooth transition to talkies. The first picture, *Romance Ahoy!* opposite Dorothy Revier, wasn't bad. A couple critics were charmed. One reviewer called his light comic touch, "the unexpected delight of the season." However, Regal Pictures, the studio in charge of distributing *Romance Ahoy!* had minimal pull among theater owners, so the theaters where the picture played were few and far between.

At the premiere in San Francisco, less than half of the theater was full. Raymond had stood and waved at the start of the film. He was scheduled to speak after the screening, but he'd hidden a flask inside his tuxedo and another in his sock garter. Two minutes into his speech, the studio representative told the sound man to cut his microphone. The film's director spoke instead. Dorothy Revier was not amused by his unprofessionalism. She demanded to be chauffeured back to Hollywood in a separate car. When Raymond asked how he should get back to town, Revier retorted, "You can float back for all I care," before rolling up the limo window.

Raymond spent a weekend of debauchery in San Francisco, burning through his entire salary for *Romance Ahoy!* When he tried to sign Regal Pictures on the hotel bill, the studio declined saying he was no longer in their employ. A second picture scheduled with Regal was promptly cancelled. Raymond asked Bernie to do damage control, but there is nothing to control when everything is left in ruins.

Raymond eventually got back to Hollywood by begging a ride from a fan. He coaxed her to stop and buy a bottle for the ride and told the woman she could tell all her friends she'd given a ride to Raymond Richmond. Halfway there, he was sick at the side of the road. By the time the woman dropped him off downtown, she was so disgusted that she no longer considered herself a fan.

Raymond holed up in his house for a week upon his return from the premiere. His drug dealer was no longer extending him any sort of credit. That was just as well. Opium and cocaine caused too many problems. Booze was fine. Prohibition was over and now everybody drank. Liquor was what he really craved anyway.

Raymond was too soused to respond to the increasing number of notices slipped beneath his door. *How dare they!* The bill collectors might demand payment and threaten action, but Raymond assumed they'd never follow through with a star of his calibre. He assumed wrong. The stock market crash had changed the way a lot of people thought. Folks no longer anticipated that things would eventually get better. That optimism had taken a leap from a Wall Street window in 1929. Seeing stars tossed on the garbage heap was typical in Hollywood.

The following month, Raymond was evicted from his home and moved into an apartment complex near the train station, just down the street from where Brick used to live. The jacaranda tree was in bloom. Raymond remembered looking at it from Brick's bed. He walked by the tree and Brick's old place almost every day. He looked every time, half hoping to see his silhouette beyond the attic curtain.

But Brick must have moved. Raymond cursed his current state. Everyone was gone. Everyone had abandoned him.

Raymond needed to get back to work. Bernie sent him a half dozen scripts. Though they were often atrocious, the scripts were still coming in. If Raymond could make it to page ten of the script without throwing it across the room, he agreed to do the picture.

Severed Bonds was a quickie of no consequence starring one of the Our Gang kids and Gilda Gray, at least Raymond thought that was her. He filmed most of his follow-up feature, *The Valiant Crusade*, in a blackout as well. The continuity of both pictures was amateurish. In the latter, the director substituted an obvious double for Raymond in several long and over-the-shoulder shots. Even his diehard fans found the latter picture an abomination.

The day before filming the low-budget programmer *Loose Cannons*, Raymond fell down coming into his apartment. At least that was what he told the producers when he showed up for filming with a scraped nose and a nasty black eye. In truth, he had no idea what had happened. He may well have fallen. Raymond expected his scenes to be postponed until his injury was properly healed, but given the film's meagre budget, any delay in the shooting schedule was impossible, unless he was willing to pay for the lost time. Just his luck. That was not an option. Instead, Raymond was filmed wearing excessive pancake makeup which even looked worse in the harsh low-budget lighting. *Loose Cannons* was the only one of his pictures Raymond refused to see, promote, or acknowledge in any way.

The Crimson Comrade had been his final picture. The kindest critic called it a poorly lit and incompetently directed effort. The movie had been shot in three days and made extensive use of archival and B roll footage. The plot was convoluted and the sound was almost indecipherable. Raymond was billed fourth. His character died in the first reel. Raymond had never been happier to exit a story line in his entire career. If he could have died during the opening credits, he would have done so.

The Crimson Comrade had no formal premiere. Raymond had to search to find a theater showing the movie. Bernie found it playing on a triple bill in San Diego. Raymond drove down for the day. The theater was a rat-ridden fire trap right across from the bus terminal. The audience was mostly killing a few hours or had nowhere else to be. Many were asleep and some snored. Raymond kicked a couple bottles finding his way to a seat. He was in shock watching the picture. Raymond hardly recognized the bloated and tired looking man on the screen. He wasn't even thirty. Raymond was glad he brought his flask. He stayed in his seat until his death scene. By then, his flask was empty anyway.

In the run down lobby, the ticket taker asked him if he used to be Raymond Richmond.

Raymond shook his head. "No."

"He used to be terrific," said the woman, "but something must have happened. I got my suspicions."

Raymond shrugged and kicked open the door of the theater. He lit a smoke and crossed the street. He dropped into the nearest speakeasy. He was out of cash and needed a drink in the worst way.

The bartender set one up for him. Raymond heard someone call his name across the smokey bar. A moment later, someone clapped a hand on his shoulder. It was Brochman, the agent who'd given him his start. He had every reason to hate Raymond. In no time Brochman made it pretty clear he had come by to gloat. "Rough times?"

Raymond should have told him to go chase himself, but he was shaking for a second drink. Brochman motioned to the bartender for another round. "I've seen better days."

"You can say that again."

Raymond tried to be cordial. He knew where this conversation was heading, and he didn't want to go there. But if Brochman was buying, he didn't really have a choice. "I didn't know you lived down here."

Brochman said he got out of motion pictures when sound came along a few years ago. "Just as well, I couldn't handle all the backstabbing and ingratitude, if you know what I mean." He gave Raymond a long look so the actor knew he was the sort of backstabber Brochman was talking about.

Raymond had enough of his snide attitude. "Those are pretty big words for you, Brochman."

Brochman grabbed him by the tie and pushed him back against the bar. "I cared about you, Raymond. I went to bat for you. I am the one who guided you, made you a success and you shit on that. Well, fuck you."

"That's a bunch of bushwa."

"You're so stewed to the gills you don't know what's what anymore."

Raymond pointed to himself. "I made myself a success, nobody else. Got that? Nobody."

"You were a success in spite of yourself, and the only time you were in charge was when it all came crashing down, then were you responsible. You playing carnivals yet? Sideshows? They put you in a pen at the country fair with the rest of the freaks."

"Go to hell."

Brochman shook his head. "I knew you for who you were the day you left Arcadia, Mr. Big Shot."

"I had to do whatever it took."

"Had to? Or chose to?" Brochman eyed him head to toe. "Enjoy watching what's left of your life disappear in the rearview mirror. And while you're at it, why don't you do us all a favor and just finish the job? The slow fade of drinking yourself to death is ugly to watch. Here's some green for your funeral." Brochman grabbed a ten out of his wallet and threw the sawbuck in Raymond's face before going back to his buddies across the room. The entire table turned his direction and laughed. "Lush," Raymond overheard one of them say.

The encounter upset him deeply. Raymond left the gin joint and picked up a bottle along with another pack of smokes. He went to the beach and finished the fifth. He was on a real toot. His trip back to Hollywood was a blur. Raymond found out later he'd wrecked his car. He sold the mess for scrap metal later in the week. When the fellow at the junk yard saw it, he said Raymond was lucky to have made it out of there alive. Raymond had his doubts. Maybe Brochman was right. Maybe it would be better for everyone if he hadn't made it out alive.

Raymond thought about going home for about a minute and a half, but returning to Reeversville a failure had never really been an option. He might have gone back earlier, back when he was on top, but he could never return now. Not like this. He had to prove himself and succeed for his parents to show that town what was what. That was all he'd really wanted. But somehow he got all mixed up. Life had become confusing. Along the way to the top, things had just gotten out of hand. When he finally got there, he'd forgotten to gloat. *Ironic, really*. The thought made Raymond laugh, and once he started he couldn't seem to stop.

14

In the coming months, Raymond's luck went from bad to worse. With a studio no longer protecting him, his bad behavior had become public scandal. Time and again he proved the tinseltown naysayers wrong: *He could get arrested in this town*. Public intoxication. Resisting arrest. Indecent exposure. The latter was really no more than taking a slash in an alley. Raymond was certain someone was out to sabotage him just like they had been back in Reeversville.

Motion Picture News ran a tawdry piece with a recent mugshots under the headline, *Remember When He Used to Make Us Swoon?* The magazine called Raymond Richmond the sheik of skid row. They called him a has been and a souse and said he set a shameful example. The magazine article called his story a cautionary tale. Sadly, the descriptions of his life were more factual than hurtful. In his more lucid moments, Raymond called himself much worse. Most mornings, he could no longer bear to look at himself in the mirror.

Motion Picture News got little to no response on the article. Apparently, no one cared too much about what had happened to Raymond Richmond. He was wasted ink. A nobody. Someone who used to be big in the silent days, back in the dark ages. The fact of his becoming a typical drunk was sad more than juicy.

The grand lifestyle that Raymond once enjoyed was decidedly a thing of the past. He was unable to live even modestly anymore. During his peak, Raymond had spent as lavishly and foolishly as a child in a candy store. Every bit of extravagance—the fleet of cars, the mink-lined coats, the jeweled cufflinks—was proof to those folks back home that he'd become somebody. Raymond believed the good times would last forever, and that the money would never come to an end. What little reserves he had vanished when the market crashed. Bad investments. Buying short on stocks. Non-contracted loans.

After the crash, Raymond fired his staff and moved into an apartment. Despite the necessary downsizing, Raymond failed to grasp the real gravity of the situation. He couldn't be broke. Little by little, he hocked what he could: the breezer and the coupe, the Italian suits, the Swiss silverware, the jewelry, the gold-tipped walking stick. Cash from the pawn shop bought him time. He kept hoping another role, another windfall was just around the corner. All he needed was one great part. Raymond kept praying his life would miraculously turn around. But the phone never rang, and the scripts stopped coming. One day, he only had one thing left to sell.

Raymond Richmond was broke, hungry, and desperate, but he was still handsome despite the bloat and the hard living. He was half stewed and sitting bar side at one of his favorite haunts, complaining to the bartender about being strapped for cash. The bartender motioned him to come closer.

"I know where you can get your hands on some quick and easy dough-re-mi."

Raymond raised his eyebrows. "Where? How? Do you know who's casting?"

The bartender slid him a shooter on the house. Raymond thanked him for the belt. He never turned down free hooch. The bartender said he had this friend. "Actually, a friend of a friend. Makes really good dough. Comes in here all the time flashing it."

Raymond grabbed the bartender by the hand. "What do I have to do?"

"Nothing an odd bird like you wouldn't be doing already. If you catch my drift." The bartender pushed a slip of paper across the bar with name Minnie on it. "Why don't you do yourself a favor and give her a jingle."

Raymond had heard of Minnie's boys. Heard plenty of jokes about the sort of service Minnie provided. Cake eaters and gigolos for a bunch of face-stretchers. He considered calling for about ten seconds before giving the card back to the bartender. *Work for a madame*! Raymond was too famous. He'd never lower himself. Besides, some picture work was bound to come up. The studios seemed to be starting a new production every day.

The bartender shrugged. "Times are tough. You can either do yourself some good or wind up on Skid Row. Plenty of joes don't have the option. Plenty don't have your past, your pedigree. I was trying to be a pal by steering you wise."

The bartender was right. Raymond had already done the things he would be asked to do, only now he would be getting paid. The bartender pushed Minnie's card at him a second time. "You're all balled up. Hang on to the card. Give Minnie a call if you wise up and change your mind. Tell her Vinnie sent you."

"Minnie and Vinnie," laughed Raymond. He said he'd remember.

The bartender added that a lot of men would pay a good amount of money for a tryst with "someone who used to be famous, someone who used to be someone."

Raymond winced and shoved the card in his pocket before downing his drink. He lit a gasper.

Someone who used to be someone. What did that make him now?

Raymond went home to another of those notices on his apartment door. *Eviction Warning! Immediate Payment Required. Past Due. Final Notice!* The vernacular of debt had become an everyday evil. Raymond poured himself a double, then another, and then another. Then he simply stopped pouring. Getting blotto was much easier when you drank from the bottle. Raymond burned all the past due notices in his sink. "Now they're gone." Raymond craved a bender to end all benders. Even the liquor store was squawking for him to settle his account. The thought made him laugh. He could probably have owned his own vineyard or potato farm by now. He'd had to beg for an extension and finally traded two Oriental rugs for a few bottles of rye and some brown. The next drink was all he cared about.

Though barely able to dial the phone, the next morning he called his agent. Bernie was in a meeting. He'd been in meetings all this week, and last week he'd been out of town. He had returned none of Raymond's calls. *Who did that joker think he was, giving Raymond Richmond the deep freeze?* As an agent, Bernie was strictly second rate.

Raymond began to shout into the phone, demanding to speak with him. His girl, Vivian, put him on hold. When she came back on the line a moment later, she said Bernie wished him well but felt he didn't have the time to adequately represent him. Bernie had decided to drop him as a client.

"He can't do that to me!" Raymond shouted.

The line went dead. Abandoned again. Even Vivian had hung up on him.

The following day, Raymond was searching for a box of matches to light his smoke and pulled Minnie's card out of his jacket pocket. He turned it over between his fingers. *Exclusive Representation. By Appointment Only.* From the looks of her card, Minnie's business almost seemed legitimate. *Starvation or solicitation.* Raymond knew what he had to do. He poured himself another tumbler of hooch to fuel his courage. He was on the ropes and running out of choices. *Times are tough. You can either do yourself some good or wind up on skid row.* Raymond lit his cigarette and dialed the number.

Minnie answered on the first ring and said hello in the low, rounded tones taught in the studio diction classes. She was aiming for cultured, but still came across as hard-boiled. Raymond introduced himself. "Vinnie suggested I call."

"Of course, Raymond Richmond. I remember you from Metropolitan. We were under contract together." Minnie said she thought he might be calling.

Now Raymond remembered her. Horrible actress. Coarse in every sense of the word. Horsey features. Even then everyone said she must be fucking someone. Minnie was no actress, but she was also no fool. Rumors circulated that Minnie knew a bit too much about certain peccadillos and indiscretions. A few years later, some very moneyed and well-placed people in this town had set her up in business. Hence, Minnie's boys. Raymond was unsure what she meant by saying she expected him to call, unless she had been talking to Vinnie. "Yes, I...I was wondering about employment."

"How enchanting." He could hear the smile in Minnie's voice. She said she was eager to speak with him face to face. "Hopefully we can do each other some good."

"Can I come over now?" Raymond took a nervous drag on his cigarette. He hated the desperate tone in his voice.

Minnie said she couldn't possibly. "But I do have an opening tomorrow afternoon. If that is convenient for you?"

Raymond said sure and scribbled the address on the telephone pad. When he hung up the phone, he sat there a good fifteen minutes wondering what the hell he had just done.

The following afternoon, Raymond arrived at Minnie's posh estate. The decor was ornate and appeared to be mostly Moroccan, French, and Egyptian. When Raymond complimented the layout, Minnie claimed she decorated it herself. "A lot of clients say I have a real eye for design."

Raymond looked around again. *A lot of clients had been lying to her.*

Minnie led Raymond into the library. She said she was pleased that he still looked handsome and appeared to be in decent shape despite the financial hardship he was experiencing. "Some stars just let themselves go," she added, looking at herself in the ornate mirror on her library wall. Clearly, Minnie considered herself an exception to such things.

Raymond knew a cue when he heard one. "You look *wonderful*." He was willing to play this game.

"Do you really think so?" added Minnie.

Raymond clenched his hands into fists. He needed a drink so badly. Some hair of the dog would undo this knot in his gut. "Yes, of course I do."

"Aren't you a charmer," she said, brushing his cheek with her hand.

"So, do I have the job?"

"Heavens no. Not yet," Minnie scribbled an address on her notepad and handed the sheet to Raymond. With a sly smile she explained, "That depends." Minnie lit a cigarette and offered one to Raymond. She said her friend Max would evaluate his performance, and if all was copacetic, they could talk again in the morning.

"Another audition," Raymond had said, pulling out of the drive in his rental car and heading towards the address Minnie had given him. The car was a final indulgence, a futile attempt to pretend he was not as desperate or completely down and out as he was. Raymond justified the expenditure by telling himself he would pay for it from future earnings.

The address Minnie had given him was to an apartment building downtown.

Max answered his door in a thin undershirt. He was powerfully built, but quite short and decidedly unattractive. Raymond wondered if Max's unattractiveness was part of the test.

"So you're the big movie star," he said in a way that made Raymond instantly dislike him.

Raymond nodded. This wouldn't be the first time he'd had sex with someone he didn't fancy. Maybe he was right for this job after all. Raymond swore he would just do what he was required to do. Max asked Raymond if he would like a drink. Raymond wondered if this was another test. He wanted a whiskey so badly, but he feared what might happen once he had the first one. The drinks never stopped with just one, not anymore. Anything could happen once he got started. Raymond shook his head no. "I'm good."

Max leaned forward and kissed him hard on the mouth. Raymond didn't want to do that. Instead, he dropped to his knees and began to fumble with the buttons on Max's pants.

"Easy tiger," Max chuckled and fished out his thick penis. "This what you want?" His penis smelled foul. He called Raymond a dirty cocksucker and even slapped him on the cheeks. "This what you want, pervert? You lousy Ethel? Go on, answer me."

"Yes."

"Yes what?"

"Yes, this is what I want." In truth, Raymond just wanted this humiliating experience to be over, but he only knew of one way to make that happen. He deep throated Max and massaged his member with his throat muscles before pulling off and then taking the all of him in his mouth. Raymond increased his tempo. He tried to imagine this was all a scene in a film.

"Damn pretty boy, you ain't half bad." Max's breath shortened and his hips quivered.

Raymond felt the sweat on the small of Max's back. He began to massage his balls. Max was moaning. Raymond knew that sound. *This was a matter of survival. He would do whatever he had to do.* He swallowed Max to the root a final time and closed his eyes. The first spurt hit the back of his throat. He continued to massage his balls until his rod was fully deflated. Raymond felt a wave of relief. He hoped that was the end of the interview. No such luck. Things were just getting started. Stamina and rebound were two of Max's strong suits. He still wanted to fuck. First, he had Raymond strip for him. *Whatever he had to do.*

"I want a show that will get me hard again."

Raymond did his best.

"Not a bad tool, pretty boy. Question is, do you know how to use it."

Two hours later, he left Max's seedy bungalow. Raymond ducked in a gin mill he knew and bought a bottle of rotgut on the way home. At that moment, he wanted nothing more than to forget Minnie and Max and the horrible place life had taken him. He washed down a few pills he had left. He didn't care if he died. He'd let fate decide. Maybe sleeping with the angels wasn't the worst thing that could happen to him after all.

He woke up the next morning in the hallway of his apartment. He remembered not being able to get the key into the lock. He saw himself in the reflection of the mirror on the flophouse wall. The hickey on his neck was proof yesterday had not been a dream. He fumbled to get in his room and collapsed upon his cot.

Someone pounded on his door around two in the afternoon to say he had a phone call. It was Minnie. She said Max had given Raymond a fine recommendation. "He said you were versatile and added you were orally skilled and fairly well endowed. He said the girth of your penis is most impressive. Is that an accurate assessment?" Raymond's degradation was complete. Her phony studio voice made made the question sound even more absurd.

His head throbbed, and his throat felt like sandpaper. He had no idea how to respond to Minnie. "Yes, I suppose."

"Well, then congratulations. You have a job." Minnie asked him to come by her *casa* in a few hours to be fitted for some new clothes and to get a haircut and manicure. "You were looking a big rough yesterday. We need to polish the diamond. If people are paying for a star, you need to look the part. Don't you agree?"

"Yes."

"I thought you would. See you at four-thirty sharp. Don't be late."

Raymond hung up the phone and put his head in his hands. "Jesus Christ," he said aloud. How it had come to this?

15

Brick returned to town following his Ma's funeral. Losing her had been rough. Apparently her heart exploded in the kitchen. The mailman had discovered her body a couple days later. Brick had wanted her to move to Los Angeles after his Pa had died, but she brushed the offer aside. Now she was gone, and he was officially an orphan.

Brick thought about keeping the homestead back in Montana. Might be nice to return there someday to live simply and paint. That fantasy was definitely an option. He loved the mountains and the grandeur of it all. However, work was here.

He'd miss other things about Los Angeles as well, like the ease of making a call when he was consumed by that familiar urgency. *Randy. Horned up. Frisky.* Brick was primed and ready for some sweet thing to drain every drop of his restlessness. After returning from Montana, Brick completed the finished touches on his back patio. A sense of completion always made Brick horny. A lot of things did. Sex was his favorite way to celebrate as well as forget. By now he knew Minnie's number by heart.

"Minnie, Brick here."

"How you doing handsome?"

Brick said he needed someone for the evening.

"One hour. Two?"

Brick ran a hand through his hair. "I'd like someone for the night."

"Special occasion?"

Brick blushed even over the phone. Minnie's familiar tone always had that effect on him. "I'm hoping."

"Well, it's your lucky night cowboy. I have just the person."

"I knew you would. You have never done me wrong yet, darling."

"And I never will. I have a new boy I think you'll get a big kick out of. I'll send him over around seven." She assured Brick he would not be disappointed.

***

Raymond answered the phone on the second ring. He had been with Minnie for a few weeks. He'd earned enough to afford a phone in his room. That had been one of his first indulgences. The work took some getting used to. He had already disappointed several clients. Due to his drinking he had been on suspension more than once.

"Raymond, I have an appointment for you."

Raymond was thankful she had phoned. He always needed the money. Minnie gave him the address and the time and said she didn't want any mistakes.

Raymond knew she was serious.

"Be presentable, and behave." He knew she meant his drinking. "This is a very special client. Any complaints and you're through working for me."

"I understand," Raymond knew if he lost this job, there was nowhere else to go.

By the time he said goodbye Minnie had already hung up the phone.

***

At twenty after six, Raymond boarded the red electric Hollywood streetcar. He didn't have time to ankle it across town. The evening air made his skin prickle and his scalp tingle. He needed a drink or two. Something to take the edge off. Hopefully, this john would serve him some hooch. Forty-five minutes later, he arrived on Brick's doorstep, a couple blocks off Sunset Boulevard. He straightened his jacket and rang the bell. A small dog began barking inside. Raymond crossed his arms and waited. He tried to stand in the shadows and shield his face. He feared being recognized in the midst of doing something so lowly, but there was nothing suspicious about ringing a doorbell. Besides, people rarely knew who he was anymore. Hollywood had a short memory, and the silents had become ancient history in less than five years. He'd never been a bona fide star in the talkies.

Raymond heard movement and a deep voice shushing the animal inside. "Amelia, quiet! Hush now!" Raymond saw a silhouette behind the frosted glass. This trick was tall. Broad shouldered.

Brick opened the arched door. His disbelief was evident. "My god, Ray."

Ray didn't know what to say. He looked at the address beside the door. His mind had been playing tricks on him lately. Was this really happening? "Please, I'm from Minnie."

Ray heard laughter nearby. Dread washed over him. He was so ashamed. He was tempted to flee, but instead asked if he could come inside.

Brick motioned for him to enter.

Ray stepped inside. "It's been a long time. When was the last time we saw each other?"

"In your dressing room at Metropolitan." Brick didn't say anything more.

Ray wasn't sure how to interpret the long silence. If Brick complained to Minnie, it wasn't his fault, but he knew Minnie wouldn't understand, Minnie wouldn't want excuses. "Where do you want me? Can I get a drink?"

Brick told him to take a seat and motioned to his sunken living room. "Certainly. How is whiskey and soda?"

"Fine, but you can hold the soda," Ray called back. "I've been storing up on the hooch ever since Prohibition." *Where had that come from?* Sometimes he found himself just saying things.

Brick laughed politely and called to Amelia to go lay down. He nodded toward the terrier. "He was an inheritance from a neighbor. Melinda, a dancer who used to live next door, moved back home to Ohio, so I agreed to keep her dog. I should warn you, Amelia doesn't obey." The dog hopped on the couch and curled up beside Ray. "She'll get hair on your suit."

"She's fine," Ray called, absently scratching the dog along the scruff of the neck. Ray didn't want to stare, but the scar on Brick's face was disorienting. Brick had been so gorgeous. He'd taken his breath away. The pearlized slash made him look rougher, more dangerous, but his face was different in some other way as well. Perhaps it had simply become harder with age and experience.

Brick pointed to the scar. "Car crash, long ago. I'm fully recovered, just this one souvenir as a reminder not to crash into trees."

"It's not so bad, really." Ray didn't know what to say.

"As long as it's on someone else's face, right."

Ray didn't answer. He was staring off into space, his train of thought, gone.

Ray's hands shook as he reached for the highball glass. The heebie-jeebies. Brick steadied Ray's hand around it. He held the tumbler as though it contained the keys to the kingdom. After taking a belt, Ray closed his eyes and said, "Thank you."

"You're welcome."

Ray took another deep drink before opening his eyes. He felt some of his desperation leaving. His color was already improving. The shakes were diminishing. The two men exchanged a look. Ray could tell Brick knew his real state, yet he didn't see judgement in his eyes. The sadness and the pity he saw were far worse.

Brick commented on how comfortable Amelia seemed. "Usually that dog is so high strung, she's jumping and aggravating my guests with all her yipping. But she curled right up next to you. Maybe she's a good judge of character."

Ray laughed. Had he already been laughing? He wasn't sure what kind of game Brick was playing, but he was going to beat him to the punch. "Well, she might be a bit off in this case."

"We're all a little off," laughed Brick.

Ray was confused by the comment and Brick's behavior. With a bit of booze in his belly, he felt less crazed. The demon inside him had begun to calm. He asked for another cocktail and drank the second more slowly. When he looked up, Brick was still staring. It was really Brick sitting there. Ray was afraid he had been hallucinating again. Those visions could seem so real, and they had been getting worse. Yesterday, he thought he was covered by spiders, and then he imagined his mattress was adrift at sea. He had screamed for help, but all he heard at the SRO where he was sleeping was a round of guys yelling for him to shut up.

Brick hadn't tossed him out on the curb. He was still the kindest man Ray knew. Ray focussed on petting Amelia as he spoke. That helped him to think more clearly. "Thanks for not socking me in the jaw when I showed up at your door. I definitely have it coming. Funny how you don't see any of that bad behavior at the time, or, you see it, but it seems okay to act that entitled. Guess it took until my twenties for me to become a spoiled child." Was he rambling incoherently?

Brick offered him a cigarette.

Raymond accepted. "I shouldn't have been that way, not with you. Those years at the studio all seem..." His words trailed off. He stared at the smoke as it rose from his cigarette. Another thought had simply evaporated. He lost track of what he was saying somethings. Ray wondered if that absence was the result of the booze or the junk. Pen yen could do that, too and he'd smoked more than his share of opium. Did the *what* really matter? His mind never seemed to be clear anymore, not for long anyway. Not long enough to make any sort of difference.

Brick pulled his chair closer. "So what happened?"

Ray stared at him. Did he really want to know? Brick's brown eyes could still see right through him. Eventually Ray answered. "Everything, everything happened."

Brick put a hand on his leg, and then pulled it away.

Ray shrugged. He was in a bad way. Fragile. Like something that had been broken and hastily glued back together, like something on the verge of being unrepairable. "I don't know. I messed up and listened to the wrong people and messed up some more. Sometimes it's impossible to stay where you are and so hard to keep on top. The day to day all of it became too much. And it happened like that," he said, attempting a snap of his fingers. "What's this dog's name?"

"Amelia."

"I always imagined you having a bigger dog."

Brick told him again that she had been an inheritance from a neighbor.

Ray said the story sounded familiar. Ray continued to ramble on about himself. "There was no middle ground. I took one big free fall from golden to the scrap heap. My headlines turned to fish wrap. I had no idea. I thought I knew my onions. Didn't even realize the jig was up until everything had gone to hell. Even after I left Metropolitan, I thought things would get better. I guess the joke is on me. I had plenty of kale. I was ready to buy the place beside The Garden of Allah, cash in hand. The sky was the limit and then the sky was falling just like with..."

"... Chicken Little." offered Brick.

"Yes," said Ray with a gulp of his drink. "The sky was falling and the market was crashing and the all of it was just the icing on the cake." Ray knew he needed to clam up. Sometimes he forgot his lips were moving. Nobody wanted to hear his lamentations, especially not Brick. If anyone had earned the right to laugh in his face it was Brick. "Suppose I could get another drink?"

Brick brought the bottle closer to the end table and poured Ray another glassful. "Help yourself."

Ray raised his glass. "Hallelujah for 1933 and the end of Prohibition!"

Brick shook his head. "It's 1935."

Ray's eyes were moist. "So, it is. But in answer to your question, I don't know quite what happened. When it was good, it was all worth it, but it's like being shamed in front of everyone when it falls apart." That was a familiar feeling for Ray. That was why he'd left Reeversville. Folks suspecting he was an invert, a three-letter man. By now, word must have spread to the Pastor and his wife. He hadn't heard a word from them since the day he left town.

Brick lit himself a smoke. "I doubt it's that bad."

"It is." Ray shuddered to think anyone might see *The Crimson Comrade*. All he had was his reputation as an actor, and now that was gone. Ray remembered more of his recent films, the poverty row productions *Larceny at Large, Manhattan Mike, The Cloak and the Dagger*.

Movies cranked out with no pride. No concern for anything besides making a buck and the amount of booze it could buy. Those films were complete embarrassments. He hoped someone had torched the footage after their limited showings. "At least they are highly flammable."

"What?" Ray saw Brick staring at him. Sometimes he didn't know how long his mind had disassociated from the present moment. *Had he been talking?* "Oh, how the mighty have fallen, eh? Is that what you're thinking?"

Brick sipped his drink. "No, I was just thinking how talented you are. Guess I always saw that in you."

Ray held up a finger and studied it for a moment before responding. "How talented I *was*."

Brick shook his head. "You have something extra that sets you apart from most of the folks who step in front of a camera, something that comes from inside. You can't fake that kind of charisma."

Raymond tipped an imaginary hat. "Thank you, kind sir." He didn't mean to sound as flippant as he did. Those words were nice to hear. He had heard so few kind words about his acting in the recent months, and even those were hollow niceties uttered by johns. Ethels that fluttered at making it with a star but ended up disgusted by his behavior. Sometimes he wondered if he had imagined all that as well. Tears were beginning to well in Ray's eyes as he motioned towards the half empty bottle. He didn't need any more, though that had never stopped him before. "May I?"

"Help yourself."

"If only I could." After another cocktail, Ray moved closer to Brick on the couch. He wondered if Brick was just being polite. He always was the shy sort. This little stroll down memory lane wasn't what tonight was about. That's not what Brick was paying him to do. "So, you are an important client of Minnie's?"

Brick reddened. "Did she say that?"

Ray nodded.

"Suppose I do call her place a good deal."

Ray remembered Minnie's warning and figured he'd best get down to business. "So she said to treat you right. Whatever you want, just name it." There was nothing Ray wanted to do more. He wanted to kiss Brick and tell him he was sorry for the past ten years and ask him to rescue him from this nightmare that just kept going on and on. But he couldn't. Something stopped him. It seemed laughable given the circumstances, but Ray had his pride. Instead he leaned forward and kissed Brick fully on the mouth. Ray was drunk and rough and more than a bit sloppy. His attempt to simulate passion was more like a clumsy mauling. He broke the kiss. "Just so you know, I'm short on mazuma so later I may need cab fare. I think the red cars stop at ten."

"We'll talk about that later."

"I just wanted you to know. I like being upfront."

Brick asked if he'd like to hear some music.

Ray asked what he had.

"Jazz, blues, classical, opera. I have everything."

When Ray didn't respond Brick put Bessie Smith on the turntable. When he turned from the phonograph, he saw that Ray had begun to undress. A sexy strip tease was typically part of the package. He took off his suit coat and shirt and had stumbled a bit in taking off his trousers before Brick stopped him.

"Can we just sit and hold hands and listen to music."

Ray had never had a trick ask to hold hands. "To each his own," he said.

Brick lit a couple cigarettes and handed one to Ray. "Let's take our time? No need to rush, no pressing schedule. Neither of us have any place to be tonight."

Ray staggered a bit before sitting back down on the couch. Amelia jumped to the wooden floor, watching them from the other side of the room with her ears raised.

Brick topped Ray's drink and added a couple cubes. "So what happened? I mean, what happened from when you left the studio, what was that, 1929 or 1930, until now?"

Ray scratched his head. Hadn't they discussed this? Maybe Brick wasn't so different from the usual peanut munching crowd after all. Folks always wanted the sideshow, the gory details, the guided tour through the crime scene of his life. *The Inferno. Sodom and Gomorrah*. Ray laughed. Pastor Adams had warned him about Hollywood, but Ray had wanted to become a false idol. He wanted the love of strangers. He'd wanted adoration above all else. He had something to prove. He thanked god the Pastor couldn't see him now.

Brick cleared his throat, The sound brought Ray back to the present.

Ray took another drink, another jorum of skee. *Lucid*. He suddenly felt so lucid. "What do you think? All fucking hell happened after I left you. I lived a lifetime in the four years I spent getting to where I was, and then I fucked up royally or they fucked me over. Depends on who you talk to. The pace was too fast and the distractions were too good. Truth is, I stumbled and never regained my balance. It took me three years to fall farther than I ever thought possible. I've fallen deeper than I'll ever be buried." Ray's mind began to fog. *Was this making sense? Didn't Brick know all this? Was he repeating himself?* Ray raised his glass in a toast before mumbling into his drink, "And I'm still falling. Destitution and skid row, ahoy! I have nightmares this pit is bottomless and so far there hasn't been much to prove that theory wrong."

Brick shushed him. "Hold my hand."

"What?" Ray was roused from his reverie.

"My hand."

Ray took his hand and brought it to his lips. Ray was still talking, "Working for Minnie, I never know what to expect. Some nights I get hired so I can show up at somebody's house and then the guys will say 'See, I told you and send me on my way. They had bet one another I was not really hustling. And they lost. And I lost too. Everybody loses when you go from film star to freak show. Well, not everybody. Folks love to gloat over how I used to be so much above them, and now I am some cretin, some palooka so far below."

"That's terrible."

Ray helped himself to another smoke. "Can you blame a fellow for wanting to take the edge off?"

Brick shook his head.

"I worried this evening was going to be one of those horrible experiences. Turns out, it's horrible in a different way. This time it's horrible because you're *not* razzing me. You're on the up and up." For the third time that evening, Ray had tears in his eyes.

"Don't..."

"I..." Ray took a drag on his cigarette and forgot what he was going to say. He smoked like he was taught to smoke before the camera. Smoking, kissing, entering a room: his instincts had been retrained with an eye for how his actions appeared on the screen. It had influenced all of his gestures and movements. "When I was at a dinner party at Bebe Daniels's beach house in 1927, or maybe it was Marion Davies's place, I met a nobleman. Count something or other. He wanted to whisk me away from Hollywood. He wasn't so bad for an older man. Trim and well groomed with snow white hair and a man of leisure tan. A real sugar daddy. He wanted me. He wasn't after a curio for a freak show, but more a museum piece. I should have taken him up on the offer, but I was a fool in love with someone else. The next week, the Count sent me a cashmere overcoat and gold knobbed walking stick along with an invitation for dinner. Naturally, I accepted. I guess in some ways I've always been a bit of a whore."

Amelia came back over and curled beside him.

Brick looked down at his hands. "You were in love with someone else?"

"Yes." Ray scratched Amelia beneath the chin. "After dinner, all the Count did was kiss me on the hand. A complete gentleman. Though I was on the level about things, the next day he sent me cufflinks and jeweled tie clips and a card asking me to come with him on his yacht to Italy. But I couldn't."

"Why not?"

Ray looked at him as though he were mad. "Because I was still in love with you."

The Bessie Smith record ended on the Victrola.

Brick's hand shook as he flicked the ash from his smoke.

"I never returned any of his correspondence. I had an appearance to make, and we were filming. Maybe I could have grown to love him. But I never had time for anything but work, anything aside from being Raymond Richmond. There was never time for us, for you."

Ray looked up. Now Brick was the one with tears in his eyes.

"I guess the Count hoisted anchor and moved on. There were other paramours, but they all moved on to greener pastures or bluer seas or younger men with fresher faces. The cufflinks and the tie clips and the gold tipped walking stick are all gone now. I hocked every treasure I owned for a snootful. I have made a lot of pawnbrokers wealthy in this town. I swear I saw Robert Montgomery wearing a couple of my old pieces."

"A lot of people got wiped out with taxes and talking pictures and the stock market. I lost the use of my hands for months, so I had to figure something else out."

Ray's lips thinned. "So, you think that makes you better than me?"

"That's not what I meant."

Ray leaned his head back on the couch before turning towards Brick. The accusatory tone had already passed. "Yes sir, I could have lived in a castle! *Sir Raymond Richmond. Lord Richmond. Count.* That was it. *Count Richmond.* I might well be a count or a viscount. But there was always you."

"You could be dead," added Brick.

Ray gave him a steely look before suddenly rising to his feet, swaying and clumsy and unsure on his stilts, at risk of falling over. He yanked his boxers off. His heavy penis swung free. Despite the bloat from his drinking, Ray's lean frame remained in fairly good shape. Dark hair fanned across his chest, tapering over the slight paunch of his stomach before reaching his crotch. Ray rolled his shoulders in an attempt to seem more sober, more in control. Less blotto. He wrapped a hand around his penis. "So, where do you want me Brick? Bent over the couch? You used to like to do me almost anywhere. Where will it be tonight? For old time's sake. I'm yours. Where would you like your film star? Don't be bashful, this is your production. Every inch of me is bought and paid for."

He patted the couch and asked Ray to quit being a fool and sit down. "Just stop talking that way is what I want for starters."

Ray plopped back on the couch. He was still naked, his penis slightly swollen. "Boy, we sure were dynamite together, weren't we? I loved having you inside me, and I don't like getting corn-holed all that often."

"That was a lifetime ago." Brick reached over to toy with his hair.

Ray opened his eyes. "What happened to your face?"

"I had an accident."

Ray smiled. "I crashed and burned, too."

Brick looked over at him. "You know. After working a long day, I used to imagine us coming home and sitting like this and reading or listening to music or carrying on. But mostly silent, mostly just sitting."

Ray said he imagined it too. He said he could be living with a count, but could never stop thinking about Brick. "I didn't want a castle after all. Not one of bricks anyway."

Brick kissed his head and said that he knew.

Ray's gasper had burned down to his fingers. He leaned forward and snubbed it out in the ashtray.

Brick said ten years was a long time. "An eternity."

Ray agreed. "Was that how long it had been?" He said it seemed like forever, "and like always."

Brick nodded. "That's true. It did seem like always."

Ray shook his head and slurred, "Ten years ago I was just starting my career. Just starting. And that's over too. And now we're both alone," he finally said, reaching out to take hold of Brick's hand. "Both alone and together." The two men sat in silence for a while. When Brick reached for another cigarette, he noticed that Ray had passed out. Amelia was lightly snoring on the other side of the room. The clock began to chime twelve.

"Goodnight," Brick said, kissing Ray gently on the forehead.

16

The next morning, Ray awoke face down on the couch.
His head pounded. His skin itched. His throat was dry.
The clock was chiming nine. Each reverberation, every
strike of the gong pummeled his skull. "What the hell?" he
muttered. Amelia was curled at his feet. A warm furry
ball.

His stomach felt like it was devouring itself. He always
felt that way just before he threw up. Ray staggered down
the hallway to the bathroom where he retched into the
toilet. Once upon a time, he'd awakened with a smile but
he now welcomed each new day by emptying his stomach.
What he once considered sickness over time had become
routine, part of the ritual of killing himself. Afterwards,
Ray rinsed his mouth and opened the medicine chest. He
took the liberty of using some of his host's tooth powder
on his finger.

Much of the night before was a blank. He'd been on
another toot. Some mornings were a terrifying puzzle. Last
week he'd awakened with his hands covered in dried
blood. Was he injured? Had he deep-sixed someone? He
smoked some dope to calm himself and instead his
imagination had ran wild. He'd panicked for hours, until
he found a bloody handkerchief and remembered having a
nosebleed.

Ray looked around the bathroom. He must be in his john's
place. His host? *His host*. He remembered Brick. Was it

really Brick or had that been a dream? Should he be hopeful or humiliated? Ray caught sight of himself in the mirror. *Jesus*. He'd wisely used an old shirt to cover the mirror in his room at the SRO. These days his reflection was disturbing. Worse than Dorian Gray most mornings. He was blotchy and bloated. *Worn as a bad stretch of road*. The circles under his eyes had never looked worse. No wonder no one recognized him anymore. No wonder the scripts stopped coming. "Didn't you used to be Raymond Richmond?" he said, shaking his head. *What are you doing to yourself, champ? What the hell are you doing to yourself?*

Ray emerged from the bathroom naked, too miserable and discombobulated to be embarrassed. His penis had slightly hardened with the morning. *A floater*. He wanted to just gathered his things and make tracks.

"Out here," he heard someone call.

Brick was on the patio when Ray returned from the bathroom. His memory had been right. *Brick*. Such a horrible scar. He'd forgotten. Ray put a hand to his head. "Listen, I'm sorry about last night. Things got confusing. I know you didn't get the goods you were promised. I just..." The simple sentence left him winded or maybe it was just life that had exhausted him. Ray's entire being ached. "Just had a little too much to drink."

Brick put the paper aside. "Forget it. It's me you're talking to, Ray. Can I make you something for breakfast? You need some nourishment, something in your stomach."

"First, I need some hair of the dog. A Bloody Mary?"

Brick said he would get him one in a minute. "In the meantime, you're welcome to take a shower. You'll feel better."

"You're probably right." Ray couldn't argue with that. The water at the SRO was always cold. He wasn't even sure if they actually had hot water at that dump or were just always out of it. The why didn't really matter.

Brick tossed him a lounging robe and told Ray to meet him in the garden afterwards. He'd have a drink waiting for him. "Take your time."

Ray thanked him. He wanted the drink now, but Brick made it clear, the shower came first. By the time Ray made it to the bathroom, he had the heebie-jeebies. His hands were shaking so hard, he had trouble turning the tub knobs. He eventually managed. The spray startled him. Once he relaxed, the force of the water began to feel good, purifying. Honest to God hot water! He lathered himself. He let the pounding water fill his mouth, and then he spit it out. The spray massaged the nape of his neck where the muscles sometimes grew so strained they gave him headaches. *Like a vise. Like his skull was being crushed.* Ray had no idea how long he'd been under the torrent when he stepped from the tub. Brick was right. He felt considerably better.

He dried himself and put on the robe. When he wiped away the steam, the face in the mirror was much more welcoming. He was ready for that drink and almost tripped over Amelia, who was just outside the bathroom door. Ray stifled a curse. The terrier followed him outside where

Brick was still sitting. Earlier, Ray hadn't noticed the beauty of the patio. The garden was laid with a winding pattern of cobblestones. Leafy vines entwined across the stone privacy walls. A low canopy of trees arched overhead, offering a sense of seclusion and bringing to mind some exotic and romantic locale. There was an easel off to one side. A fountain gurgled amid the greenery. *Quite a set up. This garden looked like paradise.* Two Bloody Marys were on the wrought iron and glass table in the sitting area.

Brick put down the paper as Ray approached. "Feel better?"

Ray nodded. "Forgot how good that feeling could be. I'm at an SRO and haven't had the luxury of even a short hot shower in months."

"Thought that would help you feel a little more human."

Ray's black hair was still damp. A couple drops fell onto the table when he reached for the Bloody Mary. He took a long drink. Like heaven. Ray took another gulp and pressed the cool glass to his forehead. A compress and a tonic. He closed his eyes and felt the slight breeze and the sunshine. When he opened them, Ray looked around the patio, "This place is so peaceful. I don't feel like I'm anywhere near here." Ray tilted his head the other direction. "Meaning Hollywood. Most of the time when you're in this town, there's no escaping the fact. We all live in the shadow of that damn sign. I like the feeling of being someplace else."

"That was the point."

Ray raised his Bloody Mary in agreement. "Well, you succeeded." Ray looked into the his drink and after a lengthy silence, apologized again. "I know I talked your ear off with a lot of piffle about Lord knows what. Sometimes when I get a snootful, I can yammer on about things. I didn't mean to get that zozzled. I'd appreciate it if you didn't say any anything to Minnie. I've already had some complaints. Promise I'll make it up to you."

Brick raised a hand to calm Ray's worries. "I liked seeing you."

"I didn't talk your ear off?"

"Well…"

Ray reddened to consider what he may have said. "Oh God, what did I say?"

"Nothing terrible. You were honest about a lot of things. Mostly regrets, that's all. Except for getting naked without being asked, nothing terribly inappropriate."

Ray recalled taking off his clothes in the middle of a conversation. "Oh, yeah."

"Don't worry, nothing I haven't seen before." Brick reddened at his own comment.

Ray took another drink of his Bloody Mary. "I can be such a bore when I'm in my cups." He saw the copy of *Variety* beside Brick's chair. "I'm not keeping you, am I? I mean, you don't have to head to the studio or anything do you?"

"No, it's Sunday. And anyway, I'm a consultant for First National now. I'm working on the new Alice White picture, so the amount of creativity demanded from me is pretty light. Not that I'm complaining. I always enjoy working with Alice. Very down to earth. No fuss about her. Do you know her?"

"No, she came along after..." Ray's sentence trailed into silence.

"Well, the studio is doing some location shooting in Arizona, and they want me there for any on site problems with sound."

"So what do they need you for?"

"I developed a new microphone."

"Ah."

"And as for having to go to work. Don't worry about me. I'm a big boy. I'd tell you to go if I didn't enjoy having you here."

Ray was silent.

"Ray, I know you're in a bind. I care about you and can see you need a hand... "

"I couldn't take any.... "

Brick spoke over him. "Just hear me out. Why not stay here a couple weeks until one of the flats opens in the apartment building I own across town? Then you can move there. But for now, stay here. I've got the room."

Ray shook his head. "I couldn't." The words flew from his mouth automatically.

"Why not?"

"I've got places I need to be." Though it seemed to show itself at the most inopportune times, Ray did have his pride.

"Like where? Your SRO? Minnie's parlor? Come on, I'm offering you a hand. You should know, we Montana boys don't take no for an answer. Now where is it you need to be?"

Ray took the cigarette Brick was offering. "Nowhere." The word gave him pause and seemed to hang in the air. "I have nowhere to be." Nowhere can be a horrible word. Sometimes it meant the same as nothing and filled Ray with dread, but sometimes, nowhere felt just like potential. Sometimes nowhere felt like freedom. "Nowhere," he repeated.

"Well, now you have somewhere to be. *Here*. At least until the apartment becomes available." Brick lit his smoke. "So, how long have you worked for Minnie?"

"A few months. And I've already been suspended twice."

Brick laughed. "What for?"

"A number of things. Getting ossified. Not taking care of my clothes and being ritzy. Not looking the part of a star. Insulting a client. Passing out on a client, literally *on* a client."

Brick was laughing harder.

"I did. Passed right out on the old fart. And then upchucked in his bed."

"What happened?"

Ray was laughing how. "The guy called Minnie in a rage, sputtering he was so furious." Ray imitated the outraged john, "Your man went to sleep on me and was ill in my bed. I've a good mind to report you and send you my laundry bill as well."

"What did Minnie say?"

"Well, she knew he wasn't going to report her." Ray imitated the client again. "'Hello police, I just hired a male prostitute for the evening, but was extremely dissatisfied with his performance. I'd like you to arrest his pimp.' I mean really. Even though that was a bunch of malarky, Minnie was livid with me for giving her a headache. Iced me out for a couple days. When she finally called, she said she was a tolerant woman, but her patience was near an end. She said it was my final warning. Of course, that was two warnings ago. Even so, I have the feeling my life as a hustler has an expiration date. In fact, last night was my last chance."

Brick said he'd heard talk of Minnie being tough. "Rumor has it she runs that place like a charm school or a military academy."

Ray lifted his glass. "More the latter. Can't fault her, though. If I were in her shoes, I would have fired me several times over. Maybe she has a certain fondness for me because she knew me from the studio."

"From Metropolitan?"

Ray nodded. "Lucky she became a madame. She was a horrible actress." Both men were silent for several moments. Eventually, Ray took a drag on his gasper. "Actor, hustler. Seems I'm not cut out for anything."

The men turned to watch a couple of birds washing themselves at the fountain before taking off to perch on the garden wall. Amelia lifted her head but remained silent. Brick said he didn't think that was true. "I think you are a terrific actor. And trust me, the first time I saw you up on screen, I wanted you to be horrible."

"Because of the way things ended?"

"Yeah. So when I saw you up there I really wanted you to lay an egg. But you were good."

"Well, thank you. Unfortunately the world did not agree."

Brick shook his head. "Hogwash. I think the world did agree. People may have thought you were a god, but you were only human. I suspect you were being overworked. Your manager should have protested."

"Brochman? No, he was too busy getting his cut."

"Well, he should have said something."

Ray said he wasn't his manager anymore. "He dumped me. And so did Bernie. Now I am what we call, a free agent. That's the Hollywood version of a leper."

"Consider yourself fortunate in that regard. If your agents weren't stepping in and telling the studio to take it easy, they were moochers. Parasites. To hell with them."

Brick's rant made Ray smile. Brick still cared about him. He was on the level. A good man. His concern was genuine. Brick cared despite himself and despite their past. And just when Ray would have placed odds that no one on the planet gave a rat's ass about him. Had Brick always been this way? Ray suspected he had, but Ray had just been so self-absorbed to notice, much less appreciate it.

Brick continued, "No one can hold up under that amount of work and that amount of pressure forever. No one. I don't care who they are. And then…"

"Talkies," Raymond muttered. "And you created some jazzed up microphone? Ironic isn't it? I should hate you."

"It wasn't the talkies that ruined you." Brick wanted to be honest. "I know for a fact the studios were up in arms and in no mood to be trifled with. You trifled."

"That I did. I trifled and more."

"According to what I heard..."

"...And you probably heard about half of it."

"Other stars have certainly done worse—roadster fatalities, abortions, battery and rape and even homicide. When everything happened with you, it was the timing."

The lecture was starting to grate on Ray's nerves. He hated being told what he should or shouldn't have done. He hated hearing what he already knew, that he had no one to blame but himself. "Tell me something I don't know, cowboy."

Brick smiled. "The point is, none of that had much to do with your capabilities. You and I know that ninety percent of that job is political. Don't piss off so and so. Kiss so and so's ass. Be sure to flirt with this and not that executive's wife. That's something I will say about you, Ray. You've never been a great ass kisser."

"Guilty as charged." Ray poured himself another Bloody Mary. "That's the scrappy Mick in me, the Irish I suppose. But I did flirt with all the wives...and some of the husbands. Maybe I flirted with the wrong ones."

"Or didn't follow through."

Ray laughed. If only he'd had some perspective at the time. He noticed the lights strung around the branches of the trees. This place was probably even more magical at night. "Ass kissing aside, I've always felt more comfortable in front of the camera. I even imagine this new career of mine, as one of Minnie's boys, as a role in a film gone very grim." Ray turned to Brick. "That probably sounds strange."

"Not really. We're all looking for a way to cope, changing roles until we find one that makes us happy."

"We all may be looking for the right role, but we're not all so photogenic." Ray tilted his enviable profile towards the natural light and smiled. When he remembered Brick's scar, the levity quickly vanished. He put a hand on Brick's leg. Here he was, insulting the man who was trying to be regular about things and help him. Who'd never been anything but decent towards him. He could be such an oaf sometimes. "Sometimes I say things without thinking." Ray cursed his need to be clever.

Brick snubbed his cigarette in the snuffer. "Forget about it. You're sure the most sensitive hustler I've ever met."

"You've met a lot?"

"Oh yes," Brick laughed. "More than my fair share."

Ray was suddenly eager to change the subject. He waved his celery stick before taking an exaggerated bite. "My nutrition for the day," he managed around the crunching.

Brick asked if he would like another drink.

Ray laughed. "Does an agent take his cut?" Ray felt something against his leg. The orange tabby at his feet meowed.

Brick reached down and scooped up the feline. "I thought those bathing birds might get her out here. I don't think you've had the pleasure of meeting Sophie. Melanie was my neighbor on the other side, when she moved back to Atlanta, I got Sophie."

Ray reached over to scratch the cat's head. "Soon you'll have a whole menagerie unless the people in this apartment complex find some work."

"I'm worried because the couple with the animal act living across the courtyard have seen better days."

Ray laughed.

"Sophie is not terribly social, but she seems to like you." As if on cue, the cat hissed in Ray's direction. "There she goes. She's fickle... which is a nice way of saying she is a complete bitch." Sophie jumped from Brick's lap and slinked across the patio before jumping to perch upon a boulder near the garden wall. She became intent on the chirping birds in the trees overhead.

"You've still got the easel."

Brick nodded. "That's a different one. I haven't been painting much. I need to be inspired."

"What inspires you?"

"I don't know. Things. People somethings."

The men sat in the garden beneath the canopy of trees all morning. Amelia moved from spot to spot to take full advantage of the shifting sunlight. Sophie cleaned herself and stretched luxuriously before wandering back inside. Ray and Brick talked about careers and their childhoods, art and travel, and seafood. Everything it seemed except their life together and their parting of ways. Sometimes they just sat in silence and watched the birds. Their connection, their chemistry was still there, but life had made everything so complicated.

Ray put his bare foot on top of Brick's. Another simple touch. Skin on skin. Promise. Desire. Brick moved his foot away.

A moment later Ray let his hand drop. Brick reached down to grasp it. Their fingers intertwined. Their grip tightened. Holding hands felt nice. Ray made circles with his thumb in Brick's palm. Suddenly, Brick pulled his hand away and asked Ray if he wanted lunch. "I realize you've had a few stalks of celery and a gallon of tomato juice, but you look like you could do with a good meal."

"Says you!" Though he didn't have much of an appetite, Ray agreed to lunch. He fell asleep on the couch while Brick was preparing the sandwiches and macaroni salad. Brick sat in the stuffed chair across the room with the new Mary Roberts Rinehart mystery and gave Ray another hour of napping. He needed sleep. The clock ticked on the mantle. He smiled at Ray's slight snore. That little snort was the same. Brick exhaled. He hadn't felt this content since years ago in that attic apartment. He needed to forget the way things had ended and remember the way things had been. Ray began stirring in a little while. His eyes finally opened. "Ready for lunch?"

Ray followed Brick into the kitchen. Despite his proclaimed lack of hunger, Ray devoured more than he usually ate in three days time. His body knew what it needed, if only he could stay away from the hooch for a while. After a second helping of everything, Ray sat back in his chair. "I feel like a stuffed olive. That was amazing." He lit a smoke. "Best meal I've had in ages."

Brick nodded. "No problem."

Ray reached out and took his hand. The two shared a look. At least Ray thought they did. He still only wore the lounging robe. Ray stood and undid the sash belt. In a deft movement, he slipped the garment from his shoulders. A slight smile appeared on Ray's lips.

"I...I'm not in the mood."

"Not in the mood. Is that why you called Minnie? I know how to make you happy. Real happy. Remember?" Ray knelt at his feet. "Maybe you want me here." Ray started to lick Brick's instep. He took the big toe into his mouth and sucked it before licking the hollow between that digit and the next. "You like that? That do it for you big man? I haven't forgotten our times together and how good it felt to have you inside of me. You always were the best. You ruined me for everyone who came after. They were never you."

"You don't know what you're saying."

Ray assured him that he did. "I owe you something. Let me pay my debt."

"This isn't about a debt."

"Then let it be about whatever you want it to be." Ray began to lick northward, from shin to calf.

"You don't owe me anything. You don't have to do this," said Brick, trembling.

"Stop worrying about me." Ray kissed Brick's knee and began to lick along his inner thigh. "Besides, I want to do this."

"Well, I don't want it." Brick was overly brusque. He pushed Ray away and walked across the room.

Ray followed him. He was still naked. His erection bobbed as he moved. Ray stood on his toes and kissed Brick. "*Please. Please.*" His breath was slightly sour, and his mouth was rough, but the kiss was full of promise.

"Just stop." Brick reached back and tossed the robe at Ray. "If you're going to be staying here, we need to have some ground rules. Number one. We were together at one time, but we aren't any more. We've both gone our separate ways. There can be no more of that."

Ray felt foolish. Suddenly unsure of himself. He thought there was still something between them. They'd held hands a while ago. He thought Brick still wanted him.

"Second. I know it's not my place, but why not get out of this call boy business?"

Ray sighed. He wanted to, but he said he lacked alternatives.

"You have one now."

Ray smiled. "I'd be doing a lot of johns in the Southern California area a favor. Lord knows I'm no good as a gigolo."

"Like I said, you've got a place here until you get on your feet."

"Are you sure that's such a good idea? I mean, are you sure you still want me here?"

"Why?"

"I don't want to be a four flusher. Today has been wonderful. But I don't want you to feel obligated on account of a weak moment." Ray didn't want this to turn ugly. He didn't want Brick to hate him. Most everyone grew to hate him in time.

Brick continued, "Like I said, the Alice White picture is shooting exterior scenes in Flagstaff next week. I'll be gone until Thursday. You're free to stay here. I was going to have someone come over anyway to care for Amelia and Sophie, so we'd be doing each other a favor."

"Well I..." Ray didn't know what to say.

"Say yes. I'd feel good if you were here when I get back." He grabbed two gaspers from the box of cigarettes on the table. He passed one to Ray. "Like I said, this wouldn't be charity."

Ray nodded. Maybe it wasn't charity, but pity was no better. Yet he was in no position to be choosy. "Okay."

Brick said if he was serious about getting his life together he needed to call Minnie and tell her he was quitting. "I'm not asking you to give up much. For some men, it's a terrific career, But for others…" Brick shook his head. "I can even call her if you like."

Brick was right. Ray just needed to hear someone else say it. "No. I got myself into this, and I need to get myself out." Brick got up to use the bathroom. When he returned, Ray was beside the phone smoking. "I'm ready." After asking for a tumbler of skee to fortify himself, Ray took a deep swallow.

Brick shrugged. "Then I'll leave you to it."

Ray called Minnie and said he couldn't work for her any longer. There was an exhalation followed by a long pause. Minnie asked if he'd found himself a sugar daddy. "*Brick?*" Ray said that was none of her business.

"I'll find out, you know." She was curt.

Ray told her there was nothing to find out.

With a heavy sigh, Minnie began her dramatics. Leaving the business by no means meant that she had given up acting. "After all I've done for you! Raymond, you know how you are. If you have found someone, I give it a month, tops. Then where will you be?" When Raymond remained firm in his decision, Minnie said that once he quit, she would never take him back. She even told him he'd never work in this town again. Raymond almost laughed. He'd heard that line before, plenty of times. Eventually Minnie said she imagined he'd be dead within a month. "You've got a death wish, Raymond Richmond, so go ahead and quit. I don't need that in my business or on my conscience. Hope you like the view from skid row," she added, followed by the hum of the dial tone.

Ray returned the receiver to the cradle and exhaled.

Brick was just coming back into the room "Well, how was it?"

"Ghastly. Vindictive. Theatrical. Minnie spouted a lot of piffle and predicted my demise. She even told me I'd never work in this town again."

Brick laughed. "She didn't!"

"She did. In other words, it went better than expected." Both men laughed. Minnie always did play to the back rows of the Coliseum. That frustrated tragedienne hates lots of people."

Brick picked up the phone. "My turn," he said dialing. "Before they installed my telephone, I would have had to walk all the way across the courtyard to talk with Todd," he joked. Brick told Todd he didn't need him to watch Amelia and Sophie. He said everything was fine and production on *An Incidental Sweetheart* was still a go, but he'd made other arrangements. A friend in need of a place to stay was going to be here. Brick turned away and lowered his voice. Ray heard his name mentioned.

Ray was sure Todd was asking Brick questions about him. Ray smiled to see Brick blushing. He could not remember the last time his presence had prompted an honest-to-goodness blush not rooted in shame or embarrassment.

By the time Brick finished his call, Ray was thumbing through the record collection in a wall cabinet. Giving Brick a wink, Ray wound up the Victrola and lowered the stylus on a Ted Lewis disc. Anchoring a cigarette beneath his upper lip, he extended a hand to his host. "Want to cut a rug?" Ray was perfectly willing to dance alone, so he was a bit surprised when the towering cowboy took his hand. In some ways Brick had changed.

They swayed across the floor as *Some of These Days* played from the horn of the machine. Brick led. Ray was laughing. Brick was surprisingly light on his feet.

"Where did you learn to dance?" Ray looked up at Brick's strong face. He was so ruggedly handsome. The scar was mostly invisible from this angle.

"I've got to keep some mystery about me."

"Arthur Miller Dance Studio?"

"Bingo."

When the song ended with a scratching of the disc, the two men looked into one another's eyes. The phonograph needle and the steady click of the revolving record echoed the beating of their hearts. Brick broke the embrace and chose another disc, and then another. They moved well together. Ray rested his head on Brick's shoulder. The men swayed to Ted Weems, Ruth Etting, Paul Whiteman, and the Dorsey Brothers. Ray sought the hollow of Brick's throat with his lips. The clock chimed eight.

Brick said he needed to start packing for tomorrow. "I have to leave early for the studio."

Ray tried to hide his disappointment. He thought their dancing was leading somewhere. Maybe sex was secondary to this sort of intimacy. Still, Ray was tired of sleeping alone. Tired of being alone. Was his neediness that apparent? Desperation was so unattractive. He wondered if his instincts and his take on Brick was that skewed. Ray didn't know what was real anymore.

Brick took a pillow, sheet, and blanket from the hall closet. He handed the lot to Ray and told him he could sleep on the couch tonight. "When I leave tomorrow, you can sleep in my room until I get back on Thursday." He showed Ray where he kept the pet food and said he'd call to make sure everything was okay. Brick said if he had any questions, Todd was just across the courtyard. "His number is on the pad beside the phone."

Brick said goodnight and leaned over to kiss Ray on the cheek. Ray turned at the last minute so their lips touched. Brick pulled back as if he'd received an electrical shock. He repeated goodnight and turned off the light.

Ray stripped down and got under the blanket. He lay on the couch for almost an hour. Sleep eluded him. Usually he passed out. Falling asleep naturally was something he'd forgotten how to do. He had a lot to think about, or maybe just one thing. Ray couldn't get Brick out of his mind. What a strong and decent fellow. A man of substance. His type was a rare commodity in Hollywood. How had he ever let that man get away?

Around midnight, Ray needed to use the bathroom. In the hallway, he noticed the door to Brick's bedroom was ajar. Ray heard movement and peeked in the doorway. Brick was stretched out naked on top of the covers, illuminated by the moonlight. He was stroking himself with both hands. Ray froze. Afraid of disrupting the hypnotic scene before him. Ray could hear Brick's light moans and almost smell his sweat. Brick spit on his hand and stroked a bit faster, pulling his balls into a tight cluster with his other hand. His erection curved upwards toward his belly. Brick pulled it forward and let it slap back a few times before tugging at his nipples. Ray remembered how much he used to like to have them worked. Brick added more saliva to his fist. An especially loud moan escaped from his lips. Brick startled himself and paused, as though remembering someone else was in his bungalow. In a moment he resumed his self-pleasuring more quietly.

Ray's response was almost immediate. He pulled the elastic of his boxers beneath his chestnuts and wrapped a hand around his penis. He leaned against the wall and worked himself faster, matching Brick stroke for stroke. Ray was so aroused watching this secret show. Usually he wanted to be the center of attention. He never realized the appeal being a voyeur until now. Ray was close already. No surprise there. He'd been horny and half cocked all day.

Another jagged moan. Brick was on the verge. His body was arching as his long legs stiffened. Ray saw the contractions across the interplay of Brick's stomach muscles and knew he was there. Ray stifled his cries as he released into his hand. His body shook. A moment later he saw Brick's fist hit the mattress. Brick's body twitched. Spasms. Moans gave way to words. Ray heard his name. "Ray, Oh god Ray." Ray ducked back into the shadows. Brick had not seen him. He was simply and quietly saying his name, invoking his presence at the pivotal moment and revealing his fantasy.

Ray realized he hadn't been imagining the things he'd been feeling all day. Brick did have those feelings for him. Brick had been thinking of him when his toes curled and his eyes rolled back in his head. *Him.* With no end to the possible fantasies he might have at such a moment, Brick was thinking of him.

Ray didn't know what to do. He wanted to leave or say something, but instead he remained, silent and frozen. Watching as Brick settled back onto the blanket and invoked his name yet again. "I've missed you, Ray."

17

Ray sat up on the couch when he heard the shower at five in the morning. He hadn't forgotten what he'd seen last night. That was impossible. The sight of Brick pleasuring himself and hearing him call his name had Ray fantasizing half the night.

Ray wanted to say something about it, but he knew any mention of it would only cause embarrassment and apologies. The opposite of his intent. Ray had screwed things up years ago. If only he could go back in time and do things differently. Make wiser choices. Be less self-absorbed. Maybe they'd still be living in Mrs. Hanover's attic apartment. Had his career really been worth it? What had it proven? Had being a star really made him somebody? Ray realized he'd been a Class A heel. He'd betrayed Brick's trust and hurt him deeply.

Ray wanted to knock on the bathroom door right now and vow to change, but he knew how empty words could be, especially with his track record. *Meaningless. Hollow. Manipulative.* An actor's tools. He needed to show Brick that he'd changed. He wanted to go back to being the young man Brick had made love to on the beach. Or the young man in front of the jacaranda blossoms. Or maybe someone better.

Brick emerged from the bathroom a few minutes later with that impressive torso wrapped in a dark green towel. He headed to the kitchen and made himself a cup of coffee.

"Hey," he said. "You're up early. Hope I didn't wake you."

Ray said he always had trouble sleeping in a new place. He hadn't been able to sleep at the Pastor Adams's house for almost a month after his parents had died.

Brick offered him a cup of coffee, but Ray shook his head. He looked at Brick's physique. He still had one of the most beautiful bodies Ray had ever seen. Tall, broad-shouldered, and packed with lean muscle. He didn't have much of an ass, but Ray had enough meaty backside for the both of them. To sweeten the pot, Brick was furry in all the right places. Ray imagined following the trail of dark hair from his navel down to the treasure beneath his towel. Ray saw the promising bulge there. Had Brick seen him looking? Ray's erection twitched beneath the blanket, and he moved his hands to his lap. Since when had he become so shy?

Brick put down his coffee. "I'd better get dressed. I'm glad your staying. It will be nice to have someone to come home to."

Ray smiled. Brick's beautiful brown eyes had lost none of their softness, none of their appeal. Did he really mean that? "Like I said before, you don't have to do this." Ray was willing to do whatever it took to right his checkered past for this man. He'd been a fool. Maybe his string of misfortune had a purpose after all. Sometimes a man needs to get smacked down to find out what matters.

"I want to do this. And you can thank me by not burning the place down," said Brick, heading heading into the bedroom.

"You got it."

After he emerged a few moments later fully dressed, Brick reiterated that he'd see him on Thursday and Todd was across the courtyard if he had any questions.

"Got it."

***

Brick grabbed his packed cardboard suitcase from the front closet. The morning was crisp. The sun had not yet fully risen, but the scattered clouds had lightened with vibrant streaks of orange and pink. The air was fragrant with jasmine. Brick drove his 1931 Auburn Convertible to First National Studio in Burbank. He parked the breezer in the studio lot and put the top up. He was half an hour early, but there was a popular saying at First National, "If you're on time, you're late." Brick could have gotten away with arriving late, but he wasn't one to use his status for special treatment. When he was an underling, that used to get his goat. He resented the big shots who seemed to live by the motto of *Do As I Say, Not As I Do*.

Today Brick had another reason for being early. He dropped a coin in the phone box and called Todd. He had been friends with the sixty-something entertainer since the day Brick had moved into the complex. Todd was good people. Outrageous. Outgoing. Unique. Brick knew Todd would be awake at five in the morning. He'd still be sleepless from the day before. Todd had developed horrible insomnia since his career troubles. Fifty years in the business from country fairs, sideshows, vaudeville, and movies, and still Todd fretted about work. Talkies had not been kind to him.

Todd answered the phone on the first ring. "Hello. Todd Crestwood speaking."

"Todd. Hello, it's Brick."

"Brick. Always nice to hear your voice, handsome. You want me to keep an eye on the place after all?

"Yes and no."

Todd laughed. "Sounds intriguing."

"Sophie and Amelia are still being taken care of. But, I told you Raymond Richmond was staying there."

"Yes. How did he come to be housesitting?"

"Well, we knew each other years ago." Brick had never told anyone about their relationship. He mentioned being in a bad relationship at one time, but vaguely and never with whom.

"Really?" Todd's tone betrayed his curiosity.

"Yes, really. This was before he became Raymond Richmond. Anyway, Ray has had a rough patch."

"So I've heard."

"Well. Ray is a great guy, truly. He's wonderful, but he's in a bad way. I don't want you to necessarily keep tabs on him. I mean, I trust him so you don't need to wear out your welcome going over there. But if anything seems wrong, maybe just knock on the door and see how he's doing. He's a bit fragile."

"*Fragile*. That's an interesting word to use for Mr. Richmond, given all I've heard. Well, if it's theft you're worried about, I'll make sure he doesn't rob you blind."

"That's not what I meant by keeping an eye on the place. I'm not concerned with anything criminal. He just has his problems, we all do." Brick found himself defending Ray. "He's not what you think. The guy needs a break. You know how this town likes to talk. People can be crucified by rumors."

"I know. Sometimes they crucify with silence as well. Fifty years in the business and nobody wants to give me the time of day." Brick should have seen this coming. So many of their conversations circled around to Todd's stalled film career. Brick had to cut Todd off if he was going to make the bus. "Todd, be a pal and just check on him now and then. If you hear Amelia barking, pop by to see if all is well, or if you see Ray out walking her, be nice. In other words, be a friend but not a snoop. I'd appreciate it. I've got to run, the bus leaves in five."

"Say hello to Alice."

"Will do." Brick hung up the phone. He had to let all this worrying go. He had given Ray the key, so now he needed to trust him. Ray needed someone to have confidence in him. Brick had to believe everything was going to be all right.

A fleet of three busses took the main cast and a functional crew of *An Incidental Sweetheart* to Flagstaff for the necessary exterior shooting. The principal actors as well as several builders and designers, Alice's stand-in, the hair and make-up crew, a costumer and seamstress, a couple of guys from Publicity, and two writers piled into the First National busses. The result looked more like a raucous road trip than a work caravan. The director and his assistant took a separate car. Typically, Brick liked riding with the workers. The lively group tended to make the riding time pass quickly. But today the hubbub bothered him. Brick tried to catch forty winks, but continued to worry. He hoped he was doing the right thing trusting Ray with his pets and his home.

18

Ray awoke in the morning with Amelia curled on one side of him, and Sophie purring softly on the arm of the sofa. Ray scratched Amelia. The terrier rolled onto her back to give Ray optimal access to her stomach. When Ray reached to scratch Sophie, the cat stretched and moved to the back of the couch where she stared for a moment. When Ray called her and patted the blanket beside him, she hissed, jumped down, and ran out of the room. *Cats*, he thought with a shake of his head.

Ray stretched, got up from the couch and walked into the kitchen with an extended yawn. Time to make some coffee. Brick had left a sheet on the counter with detailed instructions about the feeding of the cat and the dog along with Amelia's typical walking schedule and added, *In the morning, I usually just let her take care of her business in the garden*. At the bottom of the page he'd written: *Looking forward to seeing everyone when I get home on Thursday*. Ray took the note and doodled in the word *Love* above Brick's name in pencil along with *xox*.

Ray's smile began deep inside and spread to his mouth. He'd been included as part of "everyone." Ray couldn't recall the last time he'd belonged. At Arcadia and Metropolitan, that hadn't been the case, not really. His belonging at the studios had been business, and being a part of that collective was conditional. He only realized that after leaving. He found it tough to believe he could've been so blind. In truth, the last time he felt a sense of belonging was all those years ago with Brick in that attic apartment. Before that, it had been with his parents back in Reeversville. Belonging felt a lot like being loved.

After plugging in the percolator, Ray opened the back door and let Amelia run into the garden. She quickly squatted behind some flowers near the stone wall. Ray turned back and looked around the bungalow. He felt odd being alone in someone else's home. *Like a ghost or a vandal*, he thought. No one had trusted him in so long, and he couldn't blame them. He'd hardly shown himself to be the trustworthy type. If anything, he'd proven himself to be the opposite. Being asked to stay here was a godsend. He hated living in that fleabag SRO downtown. The only step down from there was homelessness. The thought sent a shiver down his spine. Homeless meant nowhere to go. nowhere to belong.

Ray heard a thud at the door. Paper delivery. Brick got daily *Variety* and *The Los Angeles Examiner*. Ray was tempted to page through *Variety* but thought better of it. *Contracts. Castings. Deals.* Reading about the business and who was making what and for how much would be frustrating and upsetting. He found it too easy to be resentful. Vindictive. Petty. *That should have been me.* He didn't need the anger. He didn't want to feel crummy. Ray took an orange from the bowl on the counter and some fresh melon out of the Frigidaire.

When the coffee was finished, he brought a cup of java into the garden along with a copy of the newest Edna Ferber novel from the bookshelf. Raymond hadn't read a book in years. The last thing he'd read was a crap script, and that had been months ago. Even then, he wasn't being considered for the part and the producers had retracted their offer. When the scripts stopped coming, Raymond had stopped reading.

Amelia and Sophie lay in the sunlight that penetrated the foliage above the patio. Birds chirped, and the wind rustled in the trees as Ray cracked open the cover of the book. After reading three chapters of *Cimarron*, he realized he hadn't begun the morning with his routine retching, although he was still a bit nauseous. The day before he'd only had a few belts and those were spread throughout the day. In the interim Brick had also prepared him two full meals. *Two full meals*.

Ray remembered seeing Brick's booze stash. He had a partial bottle and a half of rotgut, some gin, and some vodka in a cabinet beneath the sink. That was comforting to know. If he needed a snort, or two, it was there. But for the first time in ages, Ray felt content not tying one on. He didn't need to pour himself a drink. He didn't. He could just sit and enjoy the day. Hooch was the farthest thing from his mind. His hands only shook a bit. He was a little dizzy, but he could still read. He could spend this morning and probably all of today without a drink. No problem. He could sit in the garden and read. He put the book down for a moment and lit a gasper. His hands shook a bit more. The heebie-jeebies were coming on. The sun beams penetrated the trees and warmed his face. The sensation felt wonderful. By basking in the warmth, he wasn't so different from Amelia and Sophie. The only thing missing in this scenario was Brick. He wondered how far he was on the trip to Falstaff.

Ray remembered the last time he'd shot on location. Lake Tahoe four years ago. *A Forbidden Affair*. The shoot turned out to be more memorable than the film. He'd gone missing for the weekend. An assistant from the studio had eventually tracked him down and found him hopped up and blotto in the bed of a Reno croupier with dark skin and a winning smile.

Ray could still see the wide-eyed shock in the assistant's eyes when he answered the door of the hotel room. "Yes." His partner was naked and passed out on the bed behind him.

"Uhhh... We need you back on the set Mr. Richmond," the bumpkin stammered. No one had wanted the job of tracking down Raymond Richmond. Ray knew the assistant was green, low man on the totem pole. Everyone else on set was probably laughing at giving this Reuben the job of tracking him, knowing what the hayseed might find.

Ray had leaned against the door frame. "Oh really. I could use a little coaxing. Would you like to come in and try to convince me to return?"

"I don't think that so wise."

"Don't be such a wet blanket."

"Mr. Seagull just wanted me to let you know the studio needs to shoot this afternoon. The picture is already over budget."

"You mean my picture?" Ray had said.

"Yes. They sure need you on set. You've been gone for two days."

Another blackout.

Two days before, the croupier at a local casino had recognized Ray and shyly asked him the best way to break into the movies. Ray smiled and said the best way was to know somebody. He added that he might be inclined to pull some strings. As the conversation resumed, Ray let him know other strings were attached as well. "So are cards the only thing you deal?" What followed was a full-tilt bender until the assistant came knocking on the door two days later.

The assistant refused to enter the room and instead waited in the sweltering car for three hours until Ray deigned to emerge. They had driven to the set in silence. Ray could feel the disgust and disappointment of the young man driving. *Was this how motion picture stars behaved?* Ray imagined him thinking. When they got to the set, Ray had the assistant booted from the film and sent packing back to the studio. He couldn't work with that plebe judging him, gossiping, and spreading rumors, even if they were true. Especially if they were true.

Ray shuddered to recall how abysmally he'd behaved during that entire bender. He'd been a monster on that shoot. Not to mention how thoroughly he'd used the young casino worker. Ray had no intention of following through on those promises. He never did. Not with any of his legion of starry eyed young men. He justified it by saying he was being regular by sparing them. *They were better off not in the business*. He was teaching them the value of a promise in Tinseltown, which meant it didn't amount to a hill of beans. That was a good lesson to learn early.

Besides, how would he feel if one of these nobodies succeeded and became real competition at the box office? That would make him feel like a real sap. Admiration was a limited resource, at least in Ray's eyes. Helping another could be a form of self-sabotage. Best not to take any chances. Besides, if these young bucks were willing to put out to get ahead, you couldn't exactly call them saints. In not following through with his promise he was teaching those young bucks a second valuable lesson about the business, everybody uses everybody.

His behavior on *A Forbidden Affair* was more the rule than the exception. When Ray paused long enough to think about his past, his boorish behavior filled him with shame.

He didn't deserve someone like Brick. What if he was using Brick as well, but was too blinded by his own malarkey to notice? He didn't want to be an uncaring user, not with Brick. After being at risk of losing his place at the SRO, was he simply exploiting a chance encounter with an old flame? Ray felt a chill despite the warmth of the sunshine.

He worried Brick would come to his senses and see him for the monster he was. Brick was not stupid, just smitten. The latter is a temporary condition. "If Brick only knew the real me, none of this would be happening. If he got wise, this roommate or friend or boyfriend thing would go kaput and I'd be back to that SRO by Thursday... only now he wasn't even working for Minnie anymore."

Everything which brought comfort only a few moments before, now began to terrify him. He didn't like to feel what he was feeling. His hands began to shake a bit more. *Damn tremors*. He couldn't hold the book steady. The surface of his skin began to tingle and itch. He didn't necessarily need a drink. He could do without. He could ride out the urges. He'd survive.

Maybe one Bloody Mary would take off the edge and let him focus on something other than not drinking or on what a miserable person he used to be and probably still was. One drink would clear the cobwebs and snake the pipes. He wouldn't need more than that. One drink would take off the edge and make that fear and pain temporarily go away. Brick didn't find any tomato juice in the refrigerator, so a Bloody Mary was out. Ray opted for a vodka on the rocks instead. He forgot to add the celery. When he went back outside to read, he forgot the book. The first sip tasted like heaven. By the second drink, he didn't bother using the glass. The bottle fit into his hand just fine.

19

When Ray awoke a few hours later, he was lying face down on the couch. The cushion was dark and moist with drool. A burned-out cigarette was on the floor beside the sofa. Luckily, the gasper didn't look to have done any damage. The vodka and the whiskey bottles were lying on the coffee table before him. *Another blackout*. He rarely wondered what happened anymore. The blackout memories never surfaced. That time was simply gone. *Vanished*. He hoped the usual had happened and nothing more. Nothing heinous or criminal.

Before Ray could begin to get his bearings, he heard a knock on the door. Had someone been knocking all along? Judging from the angle of the sun, it looked to be late afternoon. Early evening? Amelia was barking at the door and turned to look back at him. She probably had to go out. For reasons unknown, Ray must have closed the patio doors. Sophie stared from the counter. *When were they supposed to eat? Had he slept through a meal?* The knocking continued. Ray's brain was fuzzy and his breath was foul. "Coming," he managed, checking himself quickly in the hallway mirror. He turned away quickly. *Frightening. Hideous.*

Ray didn't realize he was wearing just his boxers until he read the look on the puss of the gent behind the screen. Once he recovered from his obvious surprise, the man in the brightly-colored waistcoat introduced himself as Todd "from just over there." Todd pointed across the courtyard.

"I'm Raymond."

Todd nodded.

Ray couldn't disguise his disorientation or the fact that he had just awakened. He wondered if Todd could smell the coffin varnish on his breath or see his bloodshot eyes through the screen.

Todd looked Ray up and down and said it was nice to meet him. Todd took a step back and asked if everything was okay. "Brick wanted me to check and make sure things were going smoothly."

Ray scratched behind an ear. "Uh, yeah, sure, everything is terrific. Copacetic. Why wouldn't it be?" He hoped he didn't sound too defensive.

Todd fussed a bit with his collar. "Well, I guess Brick tried calling earlier and didn't get an answer. He was worried. You know how he can be."

Ray looked behind him before he answered. "No, everything is fine, just fine." He turned back to Todd. "I must have just been napping. I guess I'm a heavy sleeper."

"I guess you are."

Ray was going to say more but stopped when he realized he wasn't fooling Todd.

"Okay, like I said, Brick wanted me to check on things. If you need anything just give a holler, my bungalow is right across the courtyard. Number twenty-five."

"Gotcha. Will do, thank you." Ray could not end this conversation quickly enough. How could he have been such a dope?

"Nice to meet you, Ray." Todd turned and headed back across the courtyard.

"Nice meeting you ,Todd," Ray called through the screen.

Todd did a fey wave over his shoulder without looking back.

Ray closed the door. He hoped he hadn't sabotaged things with that performance. Just his lousy luck. Ray shook his head. *Not true.* Being roused from a drunken stupor had nothing to do with bum luck. Everything had been his own doing. Brick had entrusted him with his place and his animals, but his thirst for oblivion had undermined his best intentions. "That was so stupid," Ray said aloud, "It's never just one drink." He tossed the empty bottles clanking in the trash. The sound stabbed at his headache. He briefly worried the dead soldiers had been visible to Todd through the screen door. Maybe Todd was on the phone right now, giving Brick a full report. "Lush," he mouthed, eying himself in the hallway mirror. "Nothing but a lousy lowdown hoary-eyed lush."

The telephone rang.

"Hello!"

Ray was not surprised to hear Brick calling from Flagstaff. Ray said he was glad he made it there okay.

Brick made some small talk. "Alice had played a real doozy of a prank on Hank, the director. After we left for the shoot, she snuck back to the hotel and hid a mackerel in Hank's closet. By the end of the day in the Arizona heat, all his clothes stunk to high heaven. Alice had Catch of the Day stitched onto his chair sleeve. She is sure some jokester and a real kewpie doll." Eventually, he asked how things were.

Ray had been waiting for him to ask. He heard the concern in his voice, but could tell Brick was trying to be regular about it. Proof once again that Brick was a good egg, a sweet and classy guy. "Fine."

"I worried when I didn't get an answer earlier."

"I know." Ray considered concocting some convoluted tale, but decided he'd had enough of lying. That got him nowhere and only added to the mess. Ray didn't want to be that man anymore. He rubbed a hand across the stubble of his beard. "Actually, everything hasn't been fine. I had a couple drinks in the garden. Actually more than a couple."

Brick was quiet. Listening.

"I just, I just started thinking too much about things. Things I've done. People I've wronged. Regrets about the past. I've been a real louse. I ended up clearing out the liquor cabinet."

There was silence on the line.

"I can understand if you want me to leave."

"I don't want you to leave."

Ray thanked him. There were tears in his eyes. The kindness was more than he deserved. "I want you to know. I'm going to stop." He didn't know he was going to say he was quitting until the moment when the words left his mouth.

"Drinking?"

"I want to. If I could only stop after that first drink everything would be good. One drink is not bad, right?"

"Not if that's it. But maybe you can't stop after one. Some folks can't. Doesn't mean they're weak or stupid, just different. They just can't stop. If you're one of those folks, I think you're right in giving it up altogether. From the sound of it, drinking hasn't done you any favors."

Ray knew Brick was right. "I'm stopping today. Figures as soon as booze becomes legal again I'd want to quit."

Brick laughed. "I have another idea about quitting. I am going to have a couple bottles delivered to the house today. See if you can have one or two drinks a day. Try drinking less. When I get back we'll work on helping you quit this stuff proper. I don't want you going through this alone."

"You would do that for me?"

"I would. I couldn't help my father, but maybe I can help you."

Ray didn't know what to say.

Brick said the liquor store number was on his desk. He said that if Ray was desperate for a third bottle before Thursday to just call. "They make deliveries. Feel free to put any food you want on my tab as well."

Although he couldn't quite believe the words coming out of his mouth, Ray said it might be wise to arrange it so only Brick can make the order for liquor. "I know how I can be." His voice grew soft. "Brick, I'm not lying. I'm really done with the stuff, in more ways than one. I can't get my life together with liquor around."

"Promise me you won't try to quit altogether until I get home."

Ray agreed. "That rotgut undermines me every damn time. And for the first time in a long time, I feel like I might actually be able to get my life together."

"I suspect you will."

Ray hadn't expected to say any of this. He'd never given air to those sorts of things before, not to anyone. He always feared getting the freeze if he was on the square about things. He had done the unthinkable and told the truth. And Brick had thanked him instead of rejecting him. *Thanked him* for being honest. The thought of getting clean was both terrifying and exciting. "Thanks again, Brick," said Raymond. "For all this, and for giving me a chance."

Brick said he wouldn't have done it if he didn't believe in him. The words brought a rush of emotion to Ray. *He believes in me.* No one had said something like that to him in such a long time. Certainly not anyone who'd seen him at his worst. Years had gone by since he had even believed in himself.

Brick said he needed to go. "Dinner time. Besides, this call is costing a fortune… but don't get me wrong, it's worth every penny. And so are you. See you in a few days."

"I'll be waiting."

"Goodbye."

By the time Ray said, "I miss you," Brick was already off the line.

20

For the remainder of Brick's on-location shoot, Ray
struggled not to drink. Against Brick's advice, he decided
to go cold turkey. Ray dreaded the thought of Brick
having a front row seat to his withdrawal even more than
he dreaded quitting the sauce. And stopping scared him. *A
lot*. Ray had drank so much for so long he didn't know
what to expect. He didn't even know who he'd be without
booze.

The first day without alcohol he shook and sweated
through the heebie-jeebies. He almost had a drink at
several points. He even poured himself a highball, but
threw the glass into the sink a moment later. *Stupid!* He
turned from the mess. He paced and cursed and found it
impossible to sleep. His bones felt allergic to his skin.
When Brick called that night, Ray didn't tell him he was
quitting altogether. He said tapering off was going okay.
Ray didn't want him to worry.

On his second day without alcohol, Ray was as sick as
he'd ever been in his life. He was wracked by intermittent
cramps and tremors and diarrhea. He'd had the chills and
then hot flashes and then chills again. His body ached
from spasms. Convulsions. He felt like he'd been
repeatedly punched in the gut. His hair was plastered to
his skull. His head was pounding. The sheets were sopping
with sweat. He feared he was dying and dropped to his
knees to ask forgiveness from a God he had abandoned

years ago in Reeversville. He cursed and bargained. *Pleaded*. Shook. Moaned. His eyes itched. His asshole burned. He saw the deadened likenesses of his parents in his peripheral vision. He smelled their rot. When the cramps eased in his legs, he got up and looked. No one else was in the bungalow. Just Amelia and Sophie. The dog and cat stared at him from a safe distance.

When Brick called the second day, Ray couldn't hide the the fact that he was detoxing. His voice betrayed him. His convulsions were accompanied by guttural outbursts. The receiver shook in his hand. Ray lied and said the worst was behind him. "Today is a cake walk compared to yesterday." Ray could tell Brick wanted to believe him.

"I'm proud of you. Todd is just across the courtyard and I'll be home tomorrow night."

Ray let out a moan. The outbursts were nothing he could control. "I love you."

The next day was Thursday. Brick was coming home. By then, the side effects of not drinking were still painful, but not disabling. Shivers. Aches. Spasms. That day the worst part were his unrelenting shakes. *I can make it through this, I can make it through the next five minutes* had become his mantra. Breaking his day into moments helped him a great deal. By mincing the blocks of time, Ray managed to endure the DTs and the jitters. Keeping busy was key. He weeded the garden. Having his hands in the dirt calmed him. Afterward, he took a long shower. Amelia stood and watched him.

Donning a hat and a pair of Brick's dark glasses, Ray took the dog on a walk around the neighborhood and down Sunset Boulevard. Fresh air felt good. They were both panting by the time he returned to the apartment complex. Ray found it hard to believe it wasn't yet noon. *Time was so different sober.*

"Hello neighbor!" called Todd from across the way.

Ray raised a hand in greeting. The old Ray would have kept walking, but he didn't want to be the man he had been anymore. He was ready to try things a different way. Ray crossed the courtyard to say hello. "Amelia and I were just out ankling around the neighborhood. I never realized there were so many hills in this town," he said, mopping his brow.

"Different than cruising in a limousine, huh?"

Ray nodded, obviously still winded.

"You're both panting. I'll bring Miss Amelia a bowl of water. Can I get you something? Coca Cola? Lemonade?" Ray figured Brick had filled Todd in about his being on the wagon. Otherwise ,Todd would have offered him a cocktail. Todd sure looked the type to spike his lemonade with a little liquid pep.

"Coca-Cola is fine. Thank you." Just then a tremor shook Ray. An unintentional moan escaped him. *Embarrassing.* He had spittle on his lip. Ray wiped his mouth with a sleeve.

Todd lowered his voice and stepped forward. "Got it bad?"

Ray said "Yeah." The spasm had passed, leaving his face red and his eyes rheumy. Eventually, his mind cleared and his voice returned. "I keep wondering when all this is going to end. But this is easy street compared to yesterday. Thanks for asking."

"Let me get you that Coca-Cola. And for you Miss Amelia, some water. Come in both of you. Pardon the mess. You caught me in the middle of one of my moments." Todd's bungalow was strewn with papers, magazines. photos, and the assorted detritus of a long career. Ray recognized him from the silents. *Todd Crestwood*. Ray figured that Todd wanted to talk about work. *The movies. The industry. The studios*. Ray couldn't. Not now. Instead, he gulped his Coca-Cola and admired Todd's houseplants. The nausea returned. A wave of queasiness coursed through him from toes to scalp. Ray stood. He needed to get out of there. Quickly.

"Sorry I have to dash. I'm expecting a call." Despite being an actor, Ray was a horrible liar. At least when he was sober.

Todd said he hoped to see him soon. "We'll talk more then."

Ray backed out the door with Amelia in tow. He raced across the courtyard and vomited the Coca-Cola in the kitchen sink. His head pounded. He could feel his pulse in his eyes. He asked God to relieve the pain, but apparently God couldn't be bothered. Ray laid down on the couch and slept fitfully for an hour. Another fit of nausea roused him just before sunset. He ran to the bathroom, bent over in pain. Cramps again. Horrible contractions consumed him. Dry heaves. Sick as a dog. He had nothing more to expel. His face was bright red and it felt like he'd broken a blood vessel in his eye.

When the convulsions passed, he rocked back on his haunches, wiped his mouth with a hand towel and tossed it aside. Something flitted by in his peripheral vision. He hated this symptom most of all. Even after realizing the dark phantoms were only in his imagination, he still felt the grip of primal fear. Other creatures began to emerge from the shadows. Worms? Beetles? Roaches? Centipedes? First he saw only the darkness. Then came the movement. His nerves began to tingle. Phantom creatures ran up and down his skin. Tiny legs moved through the hair of his arms, along the nape of his neck, tickling his ears, his brows, his scalp.

He could do this. This will end. These visions and sensations weren't real. If he could endure this just a little while longer, things would get better. The demon would leave him. He was going to be alright. Soon Brick would be home.

Ray had to believe there would be a reprieve. If he imagined it would never end, he would go mad. He'd heard many did lose their minds from the affliction.

Eventually the hallucinations stopped, but Ray's chills returned followed by spasms and still more cramps. He closed his eyes and lay down on the cool tile of the bathroom floor. Humming. He sang a song he had learned as a child, and then another.

He rarely thought about his childhood in Iowa. Days when he felt so different from everyone around him. *Outcast. Freak. Sinner.* He never belonged in Reeversville and the feeling only intensified with age. After his parents passed, when he was thirteen, he went with Pastor Adams on a trip to Des Moines. The clergyman was taking him to get suitable clothes and hoped the excursion would cheer him. The trip changed everything for Ray. Forty miles away by train lay another world. There were so many people in Des Moines. Strangers. Bustling. Finery. Tall buildings. Noise. Automobiles. Opportunity. Ray decided then and there that when he got older, he was going to the city to seek fortune and adventure. People didn't seek anything in Reeversville. They settled and maintained. Ray never understood their contentment, their lack of imagination. Whenever he heard the whistle of the evening train passing through Reeversville, Ray dreamed of the day he'd escape that one-horse town and become someone else.

Becoming someone else was all he'd ever really wanted to be. Hollywood had made him into someone else, and he craved that transformation. Maybe it was time he cooled his heels and thought about reconnecting to the Ray he'd left behind. Maybe it was time he stopped trying to be someone other than who he was.

Lying on the cool tile, Ray recalled the voice of his mother. *A nightingale.* It was her songs that he was singing. He remembered her at the stove or before a mirror. Her soft powdered scent came to him. She died at the same age he was now. Twenty-nine. *So young*. His father was only two years older. Both lost so early. Taken from him by a God he secretly hated, a God he vowed never to trust. When they died, most people in town shook their heads and said that was what happened when a Catholic married a Jew. *Reubens. Hayseeds.* Ray hated them for saying those things. For making rotten luck into something more. For calling it part of God's plan. The townsfolk begrudgingly paid Pastor Adams and his wife to raise him. The Adams's had been kind to him. They had wanted a son. But Ray kept his distance. He didn't see what he had, only what he didn't. And he was going to show the people of Reeversville his worth. Proving himself was everything. He sought success for himself as well as his parents.

Ray was still singing a song his mother used to sing when he noticed he wasn't feeling sick anymore, and Amelia was no longer keeping her distance. She was lying by his side.

Brick came home around eight. Ray had tried to clean the house a bit and make himself presentable. Brick dropped his bags at the door. "It's good to be home." Amelia ran to him. Sophie ran into the room but watched from afar.

Ray greeted him with a smile. He extended his arms as if asking for a hug, then quickly returned them to his side.

"How was the shoot?"

"Fun. Light. Alice is great, personable as well as professional. She made everyone feel at ease."

"How have things been here?"

"Better."

Brick clapped him on the shoulder and said he admired his mustard and his resolve.

Admiration. Ray wasn't complaining, but he was hoping Brick felt something more. Ray told Brick that quitting wasn't so bad. He admitted that he had stopped cold turkey, but said he imagined the worst was over.

Brick said he thought he was going to wait.

"I had already waited too long. I didn't want to talk myself out of quitting."

Brick said he could understand that.

A moment of silence stretched between them. Each was waiting for the other to say something more. Instead the moment passed. Brick said he needed to take a shower after the long bus ride back to town.

Ray's symptoms persisted over the next two days, but eventually the duration and the severity of the episodes lessened. The monkey was climbing off his back. Ray was tempted to drink but fought the urge. He had to prove something, to Brick, and to himself. *Brick.* He owed him so much, probably his life. Brick had believed in him when everyone else had jumped ship.

Guilt plagued Ray. Guilt for his selfishness and cruelty and pride. Guilt for the people he had harmed, both intentionally and unintentionally. In some ways, the unthinking cruelty was much worse. How could he not have seen the pain he was causing? So much wreckage lay in his wake. Often, since he stopped drinking, it was as if a curtain opened to reveal moments in his life. A vile photoplay of hurt. Ray saw the foul man he had been. *Judgmental. Unthinking. Egotistical.* Remembering that monster could be helpful, but obsessing over it would destroy him. Ray struggled to maintain that fine balance every hour of every day.

Sleeplessness plagued Ray. Sometimes late at night, he heard the rhythmic squeak of Brick's bed springs. Ray recalled watching him masturbate the night before he left for Flagstaff and wondered if Brick still thought of him, still called his name. He tried to listen at the door but heard nothing aside from the measured creaking. Brick had taken to closing his bedroom door. Ray had his hand on the knob more than once. Ready to enter. Eager. Ready to show Brick just how much he'd changed. Ready to prove how good he could make him feel.

Their days and nights were defined by what they were afraid to share.

One day, while Brick was working on a painting in the backyard, Ray constructed a bird feeder and filled with it stale bread from the pantry. He hung the contraption in the trees above the back garden. Brick smiled when Ray showed him his creation.

By the next morning, the birds were feeding from it. The sight gave Ray a real feeling of satisfaction. Watching the birds peck at the hardened crusts showed him he was capable of doing good things. He hoped it proved something to Brick as well. If only Brick could see that he had changed.

21

At the end of the week, Brick returned to the studio for some wrap-up work on *An Incidental Sweetheart*. About an hour after he left, Ray heard Todd call through the front screen.

Ray had been feeling better and was genuinely happy for the company. He invited Todd in for some java. Ray was still struggling with periodic urges, but at least he had his head on straight for the most part. He was finally ready to jaw a bit about movies and the business.

"You look so much better," offered Todd.

"Thanks. I feel a lot better too."

"Last week when we met I hardly recognized you."

Ray shrugged. "People don't usually recognize me anymore."

"I bet they start to recognize you again."

"Thanks. I appreciate that." Ray remembered Todd Crestwood. Todd had been a reliable comic foil at Paramount for years, playing wisecracking butlers, flustered sales clerks, fussy customers, and nosy neighbors. Though he was by no means a household name, Todd's appearance in a film helped guarantee laughs. Comics like that didn't come along everyday.

"Brick usually gives me his old copies of *Variety* to read."

When Ray asked about work Todd said he was currently between pictures. Ray nodded. "Me too."

They both knew what the other meant, and what an absurd word *between* had become.
For both men the word meant rejection. *Between* meant *hopefully between*. Between was a wish for more roles, more picture work in the future.

Roles had dried up for Todd since the censorship office had declared war and taken offense to having "his sort" represented on screen. *No Cake Eaters, No Ethels* became a motto. The studio head was even publicly quoted as saying, "We saw that sort mincing about in silent pictures, I don't think we need to hear his type *chirping away* in our talkies." Todd Crestwood was pegged as too effeminate by the folks in charge.

Ray asked Todd how he had coped.

Todd threw up his hands. "What could I do? I know I'm a good comic. I just worked the best with what he had. That's all I can do. I can't change who I am to satisfy a bunch of stuffed shirts. People know what's funny."

Ray knew how heartless the industry could be. They could crush a person with no more than a moment's thought. Rejection in a million swirling bulbs, that was Hollywood. The movie capital of the world had also become the suicide capital.

Todd said he was forced to change his screen name and shave the ultra thin mustache which had been his trademark. "I had to start over if I wanted to stay in show biz. And I do. I'm lousy at everything else. Despite all the bushwa and headaches, I love entertaining folks. I expect I'll die doing it."

"So how are things going with the revamped image?" The thought intrigued Ray.

Todd made a so-so gesture. "I get some day work, call in some favors. I know a lot of people, regular folks who know I'm talented and can bring the laughs. They won't let me talk on screen yet. Heaven forbid! For me, it's still the silents. But I'm hopeful. I'm working with a voice coach."

Ray said the studio had made him take voice lessons as well. But his voice wasn't what did him in at the studio. His downfall had been his addictions and his behavior. He was his own worst enemy.

"These damned microphones pick up every nuance. I keep hounding Brick to make a special microphone for my kind. Supposedly, the mikes are going to be getting better very soon. That's what I heard from Aileen Pringle, of all people. I still see her socially."

"We never worked together."

"Oh, you'd love her. You'll have to come along the next time we have lunch. I'll keep you posted."

Ray smiled. So this was what it was like to have friends. Someone to just drop by and have a cup of joe. Talk. Confide. He'd never done this sort of thing before. Despite all his personal dramas and adventures, this everyday sharing seemed quite exotic.

"The past few years have been rough," Todd said, "but things are looking up. Prosperity is just around the corner... in case you haven't heard. I just can't let the lows of the business rattle me. Steady as he goes. That's my motto. This town ain't for quitters."

The line echoed in Ray's mind.

Todd added more sugar to his coffee. "Here I am yammering on about me. How about you? Brick gives me updates. You've had a tough time too, it sounds like. Things getting better?"

"You could say that."

Todd added even more sugar to his cup. "So what's your plan?"

"My plan?" Ray was confused.

"Yeah, what's your plan for getting back on your feet? You're too good to walk away from pictures. We've got an obligation. Hollywood needs our brand of talent now more than ever. You can't look me in the eye and say you don't think about working in the movies again."

Ray lit a cigarette and offered Todd a gasper. He hadn't thought much about it. Was it too soon? Would hanging his hopes on a comeback be foolhardy? "I don't really have a plan yet. Other things are occupying me right now." Ray explained what was going on with keeping sober. He was embarrassed to admit that when things got rough, he just hit in the bottle.

Todd clapped him on the shoulder. He said he knew how rough quitting booze can be. "I know my onions. The bottle has killed a lot of great people." Todd took a drag from his smoke. "Falling down is just a part of life. The wrong part comes from not getting back up. You're still young. Like I said, you look good. Just like your old self."

"Well, I don't know about that."

Todd waved Ray's self-criticism away. "I bet you're not even thirty for chrissakes."

"I'm twenty-nine."

Todd brushed his age aside with the wave of a hand. "You've got looks and plenty of future in you, if you want it. From where I'm sitting, you've been dealt a pretty good hand. If a fellow like you hasn't got a chance, what hope is there for an old pansy like me."

Todd was right. Things were problematic but not hopeless. The problem was Ray had fallen down and expected the industry or the studio or his fans or his agent to pick him back up. That hadn't happened. Maybe he'd had it too easy the first time around. Someone had always been there for him, so he didn't know how to take care of himself. When no one came running to save him, he continued to fall. He was looking for sympathy but that only made things worse. Brick had seen him at his worst and offered a hand, but he didn't offer pity. Brick believed in him. In many ways, that was what saved his life. "I owe Brick a lot," he finally said.

Todd touched his hand. "Brick is a wonderful man. He of all people didn't deserve the way his ex dumped him. Just ripped out his heart and trampled it. Walked right out the door."

"Who was that?"

"Brick never said. He doesn't like to talk about it. He's not what you'd call chatty."

Ray couldn't argue with that.

"But that old lover still haunts him. I know that for a fact. Whatever happened just ruined him for other men. Brick is a gem. And I will tell you right now, if you hurt him like that, I'll kill you."

Ray suspected Todd was serious about that. He wondered who Brick's ex had been. Had there been someone else? Was it him? Ray wondered if that was just his ego talking? Had he ruined Brick for other men? "I would never treat him like that. I don't even think he likes me in that way. Truthfully, I don't know what he expects, and I don't want to disappoint him."

"I think all he wants is for you to try. That's all any of us can do. Even that doesn't guarantee a hell of a lot. Ray, you have the raw talent. The rest of it is just luck and timing."

Ray snubbed out his cigarette. "I suppose you're right."

"How did you meet Brick anyway?"

"It was years ago at a party. We were both kids, new in town."

"Young lust, " laughed Todd. "Nothing like it."

"Something like that."

"Say, I like you Raymond Richmond. Next Monday, I am going to take the streetcar over to First National to do some extra work. Some casting people there are old pals of mine. Why not tag along? Maybe we can make it worth your while. Doesn't pay a lot, but it's easy work, free food, and there's always the chance of catching a bigger break. Beats sitting around here collecting dust and attracting flies."

Ray liked the idea.That sounded good.

"A break is what I'm waiting for. Breaks come along more than folks figure. I just have to be patient. My big break is right around the corner. I feel it in my gut. And when my shot comes, Todd Crestwood will be ready, with bells on."

At first Ray fretted over how he would appear turning up for day work. As a former star, that sort of thing seemed humiliating. But he reminded himself that only recently he'd been a down and out bleary-eyed hustler. Given where he was coming from, the thought of day work sounded darn good. He had to give life a try sometime. He couldn't keep sponging off Brick. Sooner or later, Brick was bound to resent his staying here.

A few weeks ago, Ray's pride had been nonexistent. More than once he thought about stepping in front of a train or downing rat poison, but he never mustered the moxie. Life had gone from bad to worse. He'd been too afraid to hope or dream. He was never sinking to that place again. Every step forward was a step up. No job was beneath him. His father used to say, *There is no shame in trying to do an honest day's work.*

Stardom had been something else altogether. Raymond Richmond, the star, was almost a different species. Maybe he was never flesh and blood after all, but something concocted by a publicity department. *A celluloid invention. A fantasy. A creature composed of shadow and light.* Maybe Raymond was just a lie Ray had come to believe. Ray was so tired of the fan magazine fodder he'd taken to heart. His life needed a stronger foundation. His worth was not based on public opinion. His perspective had been so skewed, but the demon had been unmasked. If Ray was to have any hope of putting his life back together, he had to accept where he was now.

"I'd like to come along to the studio with you and see if they have anything for me," he finally said.

"Then it's a deal!" Todd extended his hand. The two men shook. Todd and Ray talked away the rest of the afternoon. Over coffee, they realized they knew and had worked with many of the same people. Both shared stories and gossip about Clara Bow, Valentino, Mae Murray, Billie Dove, Davies and Hearst, Ruth Etting, Novarro,

Jolson, Betty Compson, Nazimova, Warren William, Chaplin, Crawford, Garbo and Gilbert, Leatrice Joy, The Talmadge sisters, The Gish girls, Fairbanks… "Everyone but Rin Tin Tin," Ray had joked.

Todd corrected him. He'd worked with the popular canine star once. "No, twice." Both men started laughing. They even joked they should write a book, but both of them knew the studios would never permit it to be published.

"Talk about skeletons," Ray laughed. "Nothing *but* bones!"

Todd slapped his knee. "Isn't that the gospel truth. Studio press is a bigger crock of fiction than anything up on the screen."

Ray couldn't argue with that. "The truth about the kings and queens will never be told while the kingdoms are still intact. Film companies have too much invested in those reputations and careers. But when they dump you, they dump you hard. Then it's a different story altogether."

"Amen to that." Todd put down his cup. "And I've got a back full of knives to prove it."

He told Ray he was not what he expected him to be at all. "Not by a long shot. Your reputation both precedes and distorts you."

Ray rolled his eyes at some of the stories that had circulated about him. "A lot of what you heard was probably accurate. Most of my bad reputation was no one's doing but my own. I hope to change some minds in this town, even if I have to do it one person at a time."

"Well, add me to your list of converts. And I know Brick feels the same way."

"He does?" Ray wanted to believe Brick really felt he'd changed. He wanted to grill Todd and have him relate every word Brick had said about him. Yet nothing seemed more frightening than transparency and revealing how much he cared. Ray smiled. The fact that Brick believed he had changed was no minor victory.

Ray decided not to change his name in his return to film work. He wanted to work his way back as himself and show people he'd changed. "I don't mind playing the game, but I am going to do it differently this time. I'm playing the role of film actor as myself."

Todd gave him a wink. "And it all starts next week. We're on for First National come Monday morning."

"Deal," added Ray.

When he arrived home a few hours later, Brick heard Ray's whistling. "What are you so chipper about?"

Ray shared the good news with him.

"That's swell. I'm so proud of you."

"It feels good to have a plan."

That evening, Ray had more night sweats and chills and nausea. He wondered when he was going to be done with it all. Moments later he managed to fall asleep. Maybe it was the result of giving his life direction or the cumulative effects of withdrawal, but he ended up having the best night's sleep he'd had in ages.

22

Leaving the theater after the advance showing of *An Incidental Sweetheart*, Ray turned to Brick. "Very entertaining. And the sound…" he added with a whistle through his teeth. "…every utterance, each syllable, clear as a bell."

Brick blushed. "Stop!"

"Alice is a doll. First National has another winner on their hands."

"Hard to believe it was four months ago when I was down in Flagstaff. Where has the time gone?" Brick was pleased. Things had been hunky dory between he and Ray. They cared about each other, supported one another, and were terrific roommates. Was he a fool to pine for something more? He had stopped calling Minnie's boys. Even though he and Ray weren't having sex, the thought of having a hustler come by the bungalow seemed like a betrayal. He masturbated instead. And he often heard Ray pleasure himself as well. If only he could force himself to cross the line, but every time, late at night when he heard Ray on the couch, Brick froze and all his daytime determination dissolved.

Ray was still talking about the film. "You can tell it was an happy set. A lot of that comes across on screen. I'm so proud of you."

Brick held his eyes. "And I'm so proud of you!"

Ray asked Brick if he wanted to go to the crew shindig that Alice White was throwing in her backyard. "Don't be a party pooper on my account. I'm fine going home solo. You don't need to worry," added Ray.

Brick shook his head. Alice was terrific, but that kind of socializing exhausted him. He had never been the party sort. He always felt like a flat tire at those sorts of things. "I have another idea."

"What?"

"You'll have to wait and see."

Brick drove them up into the Santa Monica Mountains into Griffith Park. He parked the car, grabbed a blanket from the backseat, and called "Come on." As they scaled down the mountain to the slight outcropping, the twinkling HOLLYWOODLAND letters came into view.

"Best view in town," said Brick. "I like to come here to think about things."

"This sure puts it all in perspective."

Los Angeles was spread out in the valley below them. So vast. So many lights down there as well.

Brick spread out the blanket alongside the D, the thirteenth letter. Many of the original four thousand bulbs in the sign were burnt out, some were buzzing, and a few were still working.

Ray took a seat on the blanket beside Brick. All he could manage was a simple "Wow."

"Yeah, this spot is visible for miles."

"Are you trying to tell me to behave?"

Brick blushed. "They figured it was the perfect place to advertise that housing development. That's what HOLLYWOODLAND was, but now this sign has come to mean something else entirely."

"Funny how much things can change in a decade." The last time I thought about this sign was when Peg Entwistle committed suicide by throwing herself off the H last September."

"That was horrible. Did you know her?"

Ray shook his head. "No, she hadn't been in town too long. She came from New York during the great sound migration."

Brick had heard that.

Ray lay back on the blanket. "I can understand her. Getting so fed up. So depressed at the thought of failure that you throw yourself from off there" Both men looked to the top of the fifty foot letters. "Having your dreams dashed that way. That's rough. Hollywood can be a brutal town."

Brick threw a clump of grass onto Ray's chest. "You ever felt that way about life?."

Ray turned to him. "Is that a trick question? I've felt that way plenty of times. Backs were turned to me right and left. Doors slammed. Disconnections. Supposed friends treating me like a stranger. Yes, I've known that sort of loneliness and despair... and just wanting all the pain to end."

After a long silence, Brick added, "Me too."

"You too?"

Brick saw the look of disbelief on Ray's face. "I did. Years ago... When you left me."

"I am sorry. I was stupid."

Brick shrugged. The wind rustled through the grasses of the mountainside. "No need to be sorry. We were both stupid." He picked another handful of weeds and tossed them aside.

"I don't know what you want me to say. I was wrong."

Brick turned to him. "You were going for what you wanted."

"And what if I told you I didn't want that anymore."

"I'd call you a liar."

"Well, I don't want stardom in the same way. I've changed."

"Foxhole promises are easy to make."

"What does that mean?"

"It means everyone makes bargains on the battlefield, when they're desperate. The question is can you keep your end of the bargain when the war is over and things are going well?"

"I can. You know I can."

Brick shook his head. Most times he found it easier to just be agreeable, but not now. Not about this. "I don't know that you've changed. I'd like to think so, but I don't know."

He could see the hurt on Ray's face.

Brick got up. "Don't pay any attention to me, I'm just tired. Screenings and all that, you know?"

23

After four months, Ray still enjoyed the daily trek to the studio with Todd. At first he was ashamed and passed beneath the entryway arches with his eyes to the ground. The experience was humbling, but humility can be a good thing. By the end of the first week, his embarrassment had passed. This was a tough business. *No one cared*. Once Ray made peace with the fact that he was basically starting over, he began to get hired for crowd scenes. Ray couldn't believe he was actually working. He thought he'd alienated everyone in town.

It had taken a few months, but Ray was working steadily as an extra and sometimes as a bit player. He was in good company. He ran into Louise Brooks and Mae Marsh working as extras on more than one occasion. Kindred spirits. Once some of his former workmates saw his attitude had changed and that he and the bottle had parted ways, he started getting work in actual supporting roles. He recalled the first time he shared the news with Brick.

When he came home that day, he shouted to Brick in the kitchen. "I got a real role. Six lines." Ray picked up Amelia and spun her around the kitchen. "And hey, I need to call Minnie and tell her she was wrong. I am working in this town again."

Brick laughed and offered Ray a lemonade. "Tell me about the role."

Ray lit a smoke and handed a second to Brick. "The picture is called *Violent Hours*. Just a cop programmer over at Crescent Studios. But I have six lines. Six glorious lines of dialogue. I play a crooked cop who takes money from racketeers."

"Lowdown sort. A bad guy."

"The worst. But I get mine. I get double crossed by the *real* bad guy."

"Death scene?"

Ray shook his head and did a mock faint back upon the couch. "Nah. I die off screen, but they talk about my death... a lot." Ray had never been this enthused before, even when he had landed starring roles. He'd never appreciated his good fortune. And even though he and Brick weren't a couple, Ray never had anyone to share his good news with before. As a result, his achievements tended to be hollow ones.

During another two week stretch, Ray filmed four small speaking parts. More work was on the horizon. His charm and charisma before the camera hadn't dimmed. If anything, they were deepened by his experience and enhanced by his sobriety. Ray was a quick study with dialogue and an expert at hitting his mark. He made a convincing thug. Since the Depression and the success of *Little Caesar*, *The Public Enemy*, and *Scarface*, underworld pictures had become lucrative and gangster roles were plentiful. Crime and musicals were the hot tickets.

Ray's career was nowhere near where it had once been. He didn't have an exclusive contract or even an agent, but he was definitely on the right path and moving upward. He learned gratitude quickly and said thank you to everyone from grips to script girls. Giving thanks was something he'd neglected his first go around in Hollywood. He thought he'd done it all himself. He'd been wrong.

Every role Ray was given was a step up from where he had been. He'd been a bum and a man without a future. He'd been ready to cash it all in. Life at the bottom had been a nightmare. *Lonely. Hopeless. Vile.* Brick had brought him back from the brink. Ray reminded himself daily that he owed all this to Brick. That was something else Ray vowed never to forget.

24

One afternoon, Brick came home with his stride extra wide. He was excited. Studio execs were casting a great new part. As a senior sound advisor at the studio, Brick called in a few favors and got Ray an audition. When he came home, Ray was on the couch reading. He looked like a different person than the down and out party favor who had knocked on his door several months ago.

Ray saw Brick's grin. *Those dimples.* "What?"

"I have some news for you."

"Do you now?"

Brick took a seat beside him on the sofa. "There is a role in a new movie that I think you would be perfect for."

"Me?"

"Yes, you."

Ray threw up his arms. "I'd be great in a lot of them, but I need to get a reading."

"Not a problem. Special delivery." Brick tossed a few pages of script onto Ray's lap. "They're going to see you."

Ray's voice rose an octave. "What?"

Brick gestured towards the script. "I know some pals in casting. I presented you as an option and said you would probably be interested."

"What did they say?"

Brick laughed. "They said yes. They are excited to have you read, and with good reason. You would be perfect in this part. Production is starting soon, and you audition for it in two days."

Ray was beside himself. "I don't know what to say. You've done so much for me already. Why?"

"Because I care." Brick was blushing.

That blush said it all.

"I didn't do all that much. I mentioned you. "They remember your pictures and your talent. You have a number of fans out there, you know."

"Are you one of them?"

"What do you think?"

Ray lit a cigarette. "So tell me about the project."

"The picture is an A production tentatively called *Beyond the Pale*," Brick explained. "It's a drama about the women at home and soldiers returning to the home front after the war. Originally they wanted Helen Twelvetrees as the lead, but I heard she became too demanding."

"There are rumors about her attitude, but I'm trying not to cast stones. I'm sure I was worse."

"Instead, they went with Kay Francis, and they are looking at Rod LaRoque or Warner Baxter for the romantic male lead."

"Solid cast so far."

"And Victor Petrovich is directing."

"Holy smokes!" Ray whistled through his teeth. After coming to the U.S. ten years ago from Hungary, Victor Petrovich had become one of the top talents behind the camera in Tinseltown. Folks considered him an actor's director, the kind of artist everyone in Hollywood dreams of working with.

"Like I said, this is being slated as a class production. The part you're reading for is the second lead, Eddie Marshall. Eddie is a former Park Avenue playboy. Money. Dash. The whole bit. Eddie is the life of the party, always looking for a fresh thrill."

Ray laughed and picked a bit of tobacco from his tongue. "Can't imagine why you thought I'd be right for this part."

"…After being jilted by Kay, Eddie figures he'll show her, and he goes on a bender and ends up enlisting in the army. The war effort escalates, and before he knows it, Eddie is sent to the front. For six months, he endures the horrors of war. When peace is finally declared, he returns to New York a changed man."

"Scenery chewing?"

"You bet. Haunted by the memories of the carnage he has seen, Eddie throws himself back to his old frivolous life of drinking and carousing, desperate to forget."

Ray exhaled a column of smoke towards the ceiling. "Poor sap, I know how that is.".

Brick grabbed a cigarette for himself and read from page one of the printed studio script sheet before him. "On New Year's Eve, Eddie joins his old Park Avenue cronies at the rooftop party in a swanky high rise. His drinking escalates, and his friends warn him to slow down on the sauce. Eddie disregards their pleas. Seeing the fireworks exploding across the nighttime sky, Eddie cowers at the booms and flashes. His mind returns to the trenches. Eddie realizes he will never be free of the horrors of war and the memories of frontline combat. With an anguished scream, Eddie throws himself from the balcony." Brick put down the sheet. "His death ushers in a big scene for Kay grieving and eventually going into nursing war veterans where she finds true love in the arms of either Mr. Baxter or LaRoque. Eddie is the second lead, but it is a very showy key part, and you could bring a real depth to the role of a man who has been through the hell of war. Your read is the scene on the terrace leading up to Eddie's death."

Ray snubbed out his smoke. "So, they are cutting right to the chase."

"Well, it's pivotal. If the actor playing Eddie can't make that scene work, there's no point in casting him."

"True." Ray was both thrilled and terrified at the chance for a solid role in an A production. *Would they want him? Was he considered too high a risk? What if he flubbed the audition? What if someone else was better, or better connected?* To be so close to a comeback and then have it snatched away would be terrible. Ray still wasn't great at dealing with disappointment. He couldn't be overly confident. Casting agents were probably pitching half their clients for this picture. Everyone wanted to work with Kay this year, and everyone always wanted to work with Petrovich. "Do you really think I'd stand a chance of landing the part?"

Brick took his hand. "Yes, I think you stand a chance."

That felt so nice. Ray smiled. "I just don't want to be disappointed, or to disappoint you."

Brick shook his head. "If you never want to be disappointed, you picked the wrong line of work. And as for me, I've been disappointed before. Don't you worry about me."

Ray nodded. No doubt he was a big part of those disappointments, but he wasn't going to let guilt about the past ruin this moment. Ray was so pleased to be holding Brick's big and calloused hand. Strong hands. Capable hands. "One day roles and bit parts in programmers are one thing, but would execs be willing to trust me with more? Won't the studio remember?"

"With this performance, you could make them forget."

"Do you really think I could?"

"After seeing you kick the sauce, I'm convinced you can do anything you set your mind to." Brick leaned closer.

Ray tilted his head. "Anything."

They kissed lightly. Tentatively. Brick held the side of Ray's face. His thumbs brushed his cheeks. The kisses became stronger, surer, more demanding.

Brick stood, lifting Ray in his arms. Ray protested, saying he was too heavy, but it was all a ruse. Brick was the strongest man he knew. Nothing felt better than being in his arms. Brick shushed Ray with one kiss and then another as he carried Ray into the bedroom. Ray buried his face in Brick's shoulder. His heart was beating with excitement. Anticipation. This dream was coming true, just when he thought it would never happen.

Brick tossed Ray onto the bed. He pulled off his shirt and tossed it aside. Ray glimpsed his impressive physique. Furry. Muscled. Veins coursed through the bulge of his biceps. The plates of his chest were solid. Defined. Ray could see the defined "vee" just above the lip of his trousers. Brick kicked off his shoes and yanked his pants and boxers down with one motion. His member already pointed skyward. He told Ray to get shuck his clothes. "I don't want to see a stitch on you. Turn over, let me see all of you."

Ray flipped onto his stomach.

Brick began stroking himself. Ray heard him whisper, "Nice."

Ray hoped he was remembering how good it had been between them, and how good it was going to be again. He'd waited so long.

As if on cue, Brick echoed his words. "I've waited so long. Until the time was right."

"Is the time right?"

"I don't care anymore," Brick was on top of him. His weight felt so good. "I've been fighting this urge for weeks, months. Ever since you first came back to me. Maybe the time will never be right." Brick kissed the back of Ray's neck, licking the crease along his collar line. Nibbled his neck. Brick had remembered.

That drove Ray wild.

Brick began planting kisses down his back… one vertebrae at a time. Something else that had made Ray wild with desire.

Ray felt himself writhing even before Brick arrived at the rise at the small of his back. Brick bent lower.

"Yes," whispered Ray. He knew what was coming.

Brick licked along Ray's crack, back and again, spreading. Deeper. His tongue flicked across his hole. Again. Ray moaned. Brick reached beneath and lifted him to his knees. A better angle to loosen him. Brick slapped each cheek.

Brick whispered, "Tell me you want me."

"I want you. I want you inside."

"That's my good boy. That's what I like to hear." Brick's guttural voice was more growl than response. Reassuring and sinister and filled with promise.

Ray began to stroke himself. His penis felt like steel. Brick drove his tongue deeper and then retreated. He added a finger, then two. Ray was mad with desire, with wanting Brick inside him.

Ray grabbed Brick. "Now. I want you now."

Brick gave another stinging slap to Ray's ass. "You'll wait until I'm ready, and then I'm going to fuck you like you've never been fucked. I'm going to fuck you for leaving me and I'm going to fuck you for coming back and I'm going to fuck you for loving me again."

Ray quivered at the thought. *Anticipation*. He felt Brick's thick organ brush against him as Brick continued to feed. Brick wasn't the only one who had been fighting urges. Ray had waited just as long for this evening, for what was to come. He told Brick so.

Brick slapped him on the ass. "I know."

A moment later, Brick was ready. Ray felt the mattress shift as Brick knelt behind him. Brick spit on his hand and kept loosening him with a finger. He lubricated himself with a glob of spit and eased the tip of his erection into the tight muscled ring. Once he felt the head slip in, Brick pushed the shaft inside with a single thrust. Ray gasped. Brick was so big, so wide. *Immense. Everything.* Ray felt like he was being torn apart and simultaneously reassembled. Shock became pain and pain segued into pleasure. Every phase of sensation was so intense.

Brick began to move, slowly at first. Almost imperceptible. More. Rotating hips. Ray backed into him. Undulating into each thrust. He wanted more. Brick was ready to give it to him. He started to thrust. The simple motion became a rolling wave that consumed them both. That caused them to move as one, The result was better than either had imagined. Worth the wait. Brick grabbed Ray's hips and began slamming into him. Harder. Primal. Hands moving to Ray's sweating neck, struggling for a grip as they pulled him back. Ray backing onto Brick with equal force. Meeting his thrust with a push. Brick slapping his behind. Cheeks red from his hands. Ghosts of his prints fading white.

Ray could not recall the last time he'd been willing to so completely give himself to a man. Actually, he could remember. The answer was easy. It had been years ago, with Brick. Sex had always been something more with Brick. No one else ever felt like this. Not simply immense. More than size. Scope. He'd had a couple men who were larger, but they hadn't made him feel complete. They hadn't made him feel this and filled him inside and out. Brick was perfect. Being with him was a dimension beyond dimension.

How had they ever survived apart? How had they ever endured without this? There *was* nothing else. No other moment. This was always and everything. Ray didn't need anything more.

Brick retreated and flipped Ray onto his back. He held a foot in each hand. Ray was a wishbone. Brick positioned himself and entered again. Perfection from a new perspective. Heaven from a different angle. Hips rolled. Loose. Agile. Brick driving himself into Ray again and again. Ray looked into those beautiful brown eyes. Timeless. Eternal. He could willingly drown in those soulful pools.

Ray was so close. So ready. A moment more. Tingling. He was so in the moment that he felt a million miles away. Sex brought him home and took him elsewhere. Especially sex with Brick. He recognized the familiar combination of sensation and numbness as he approached release. His hips rose. Brick hitting him just right again and again. Ray was there. On the edge. Then the explosion. Back arching. Neck strained. Screaming. Was he?

"Let me see it," whispered Brick.

Ray let himself go.

Brick reached down and scooped some ejaculate and stroked him some more. Ray thrashed and protested. *Too sensitive.* Brick maintained his manipulations. Ray refused to soften. Not again. *Again?* Brick gripped him tighter, "Give me more. Give me every bit of it."

Ray's fist pounded the mattress.

Again.

As he felt himself release, Brick's body began to tense. The veins of his arms became rising rivers along the plates of his chest. Blood coursing through him like a creature possessed, like a man in lust. *Transformed. A beast of ecstasy.* Brick moaned so deep Ray felt the vibration along his scalp. The sound grew. Brick didn't give a good goddamn about any neighbors.

Ray felt the explosion and the wave of Brick's desire pulse inside him. Another eruption. Successors of lessening intensity. The warming sensation of pleasing his man was a feeling he could never take for granted. Especially now. Especially now that they were together again.

Completion.

Being with Brick again had larger repercussions for Ray. He felt all his dark moments being purged. As though some sort of baptism were renewing him, taking him from so many sordid places in his past and depositing him here, on the mattress, beneath his man. Making love had relieved him of so many things that had been hurting him for so long. Tonight Ray had been turned inside out. His secrets had been exposed not for scrutiny, but so those fears could be brought to light and purified by something greater... by love.

When he came back into his body he was smoking and Brick was stroking his back, telling him it would be all right. Nothing was going to harm him now. Ray realized he'd been crying. He wasn't sure why. "I'm sorry," he had said.

Brick pulled Ray's head to his hirsute chest. "There's nothing to be sorry for. All is past. All is forgiven." Brick was reassuring. Kissing the top of his head. Rubbing his arms. Holding him tighter. Ray felt like crying some more. He was so fortunate. Brick was quite a fella.

Ray could hear his heartbeat, consistent and comforting and a mirror of his own

In the moonlight, Brick gently played with Ray's inky hair. After a bit, Brick kissed him on the forehead and whispered, "I'll never let you go again."

All Ray needed was someone to remind him of who he really was. Brick held him tighter. Ray knew, without a doubt, that Brick was that man.

25

Ray was on the couch running his lines for the audition. He looked up when he heard Brick enter the room.

"How's it coming along?" Brick asked.

Ray smiled. "Everything's jake! This role feels so right to me." He lit a fag. "You think audiences will be willing to forgive?"

Brick assured him that was the case. "Since all hell broke loose with the market crash, people have learned to forgive. They understand hard times and being on the wrong side of the eight ball. And you know studio executives, they have their eyes on the kale. They may talk a big game, but they love whatever audiences love."

Ray wanted to believe Brick. The thought of a return was a thrill, but it also terrified him. Ray had expected a real role to come along, only not so soon. His doubts made him feel guilty. He was lucky. Todd had been trying to stage a comeback for years and still only got crowd scenes and a double-take here and there. He still hadn't been given a single line to speak. Louise Brooks never got more than bit parts. She told Ray she was ready to toss it all and head to New York. Louise was more talented, more deserving. Smarter. Then Ray remembered that Tinseltown didn't work that way. Hollywood doesn't play fair, it only deals in opportunities.

Brick kissed Ray, and said that he was going to be fine.

"I need to be more than fine."

"You don't *need* to be anything. If it's meant to be, it will happen."

Ray wondered what he had done to deserve this man. He was sitting pretty. He had so much to be grateful for.

Brick said he was going to make dinner.

Ray picked up the audition pages and read through it yet again.

Eddie's old cronies try to get him in the spirit and celebrate the New Year. Instead of being lighthearted, Eddie drinks to excess, becoming inebriated and morose.

Ray felt the same pang of recognition as when he'd first read those lines. He could make this role work. He was intimate with that despair. That grim place of hopelessness. He knew all about feeling unable to continue through the pain. Wanting simply to escape. Cognizant only of the hell life had become. Ray knew what it meant to see the futility of the future. Seeing tomorrow as only more of the same. More sickness and survival. More pain. He remembered the bleakness of another morning when life seemed to have no purpose aside from hollowing out what was left of his insides. Ray knew what it was like to pray for numbness. Silence. Reprieve. He could draw from that experience.

Scene 16C

*Exterior - Penthouse Terrace. The crowd is festive with
the holidays. Eddie is almost incoherently drunk.*

*Shot of Marion (Ms. Francis) with a look of disapproval at
Eddie's sloppiness.*

Fireworks begin to burst in the sky.

Revelers cheer.

More fireworks continue to explode.

Revelers begin the countdown to the New Year.

*The camera pans through the crowd to a close-up on
Eddie. He freezes at the explosions. His eyes widen in the
flashes of light from the sky.*

The crowd continues to count down, "4-3-2-1."

*More fireworks explode and horns are sounded. Couples
embrace and smooch in a welcome to the New Year.*

*Eddie looks up to the illuminated sky, wild eyed and in a
panic.*

*Eddie: They're everywhere. Always. I am and always will
be a prisoner. No matter where I go, it never ends. No
escape. None. The sights, the sounds, the smells, the hell
of it. Roger and Tom and Nagel gone in a single
explosion. The look in their eyes the moment before. The*

look in their eyes when they realized they were going to die. So many gone. No more than boys. Broken boys asking for help. Seeing them and the explosions and the crack of gunfire again and again, invading my dreams and my days. The stink of death and rot never goes away. No more than boys. There is no New Year, only that year, no now, only then - only that hell, always. I can't...

His fear fades and a look of resolve is suddenly apparent in Eddie's eyes.

A shot of Marion through the crowd as she sees Eddie approach the ledge. As she sees what is about to happen a moment before it occurs.

Eddie: Forgive me Mother, forgive me God.

Cut to Marion. Knowing what is happening.

Eddie hurls himself from the balcony.

Close up of Marion's panicked face. Revelers run and look to his broken form on the sidewalk twenty stories below. The crowd parts. Marion looks down horrified. Her mouth opens, but her screams are drowned out by the ongoing burst of fireworks above.

Marion: No! Eddie!

End scene.

Ray knew he could really sink his teeth into this role.

That night Ray couldn't sleep. Unable to put the brakes on his mind. The fears and fantasies about being back at the studio were unrelenting. Scenarios. Resolutions. Old rivalries. He finally fell asleep around dawn. The next day, Ray resumed his study of the scene. He had to be perfect. He considered a snort to take off the edge, but reconsidered. What was he thinking?

Ray pushed the thought from his mind. He studied the lines and thought about Eddie backward and forward. That feeling of hopelessness, of being haunted, of unending torment never ending. He'd felt all of those things, but lacked the nerve to end it all, at least with such a grand flourish. Ray was less cinematic than Eddie. He had been killing himself slowly with booze, but that brand of subtle demise never plays in Cincinnati.

The night before his audition, Ray sat on the patio and went over the scene one last time. Afterward, Amelia sat in his lap. He petted her with his eyes closed. He could do nothing more to prepare. He could only pray for the best. This was either going to happen or it wasn't. From here on out, this was about accepting the outcome whatever it might be. Knowing he had done his best, he would be okay with whatever happened. He must have been dozing. When he opened his eyes, Brick was standing before him with a cup of tea.

"You feel confident about it?"

Ray offered a half smile. "As confident as an actor can be, I suppose."

"You'll be great."

"Actors are known for huge egos, not unbridled confidence. I'm just going to go in there and do my best and say a prayer for the right outcome." He took Brick's hand. "Thank you for this chance, on top of everything else. I hope I don't embarrass you."

Brick gave him a long kiss. "As long as you get up and try, you can never embarrass me. You'll be perfect in the role. And you'll be perfect if you don't get this role."

Ray loved him for saying that. Brick always knew the right thing to say.

"Come on, I know a way to relieve tension." Brick pulled Ray to his feet and then onto his lap. Ray felt the beginnings of Brick's desire.

"Oh, I suppose," he laughed.

Brick kissed a trail down Ray's throat.

Ray felt goosebumps.

Unbuttoning Ray's shirt, Brick reached inside and found his nipples. Pulling. Gently, harder. Ray felt his control slipping away. He heard himself moan before he realized he was making a sound.

Brick continued to strip Ray, kissing him as each new bit of skin was revealed. A shoulder. An armpit. A hip. A thigh.

As he continued his patchwork of kisses, Ray thanked him for so many things. The audition. Letting him stay. Keeping him sober.

Brick put a finger to his lips. "We saved each other. But it was mostly you. You saved yourself by giving up the bottle."

"You gave me reason. You made me believe I was worth saving." Now it was Ray's turn to undress the man he loved. He unbuttoned Brick's shirt and kissed along his collar bone, lighter and then harder along the upper border of his chest. Ray throbbed against Brick's thigh.

Brick licked his ear. "Show me how much you want it." Brick reached down. Spanking and then squeezing each firm fuzzy globe.

Ray fumbled with Brick's trousers, opening them one button at a time. Each button a bit closer to something wonderful. Ray slipped a hand inside the fly of Brick's boxers.

Brick pushed him back. He wanted Ray to say it. To beg. To declare his desire. To put his want into words. "Say it."

"I want to suck you."

"Change of plans," smiled Brick, leaning forward. "That's my territory this time."

Ray used his erection to slap either side of Brick's face. Knowing what his man wanted and teasing him. The moment he stopped, Brick consumed him. Taking it in just

a bit and then swallowing it completely. Retreating.
Licking along the underside. A moan escaped Ray, words
followed. "You make me sane," he managed.

Ray started moving his hips. Brick stilled him with a hand.
He hefted Ray's nuts, tonguing them, coating them with
spit. "Like that?"

Ray nodded.

"I said, do you like that?'"

"Yes."

Satisfied, Brick returned to sucking. Ray could tell Brick
was lost in the process, focussed only on consuming and
pleasuring Ray and ultimately drawing out his reward.
That wouldn't be long. Ray was so close. Too close. Not
now. Not yet. He managed to get Brick to slow down. He
didn't want it this way. Brick knew what he wanted, what
Ray always wanted.

Ray already felt as though they had spent a lifetime
together, more than a lifetime, forever. Nothing existed
outside of this bungalow and the world they had created.
Ray kissed him. He tasted his manhood on Brick's mouth.
He kissed him deeper. *Yes, that was him that he tasted.*
Part of us has become one. I am Brick and Brick is me.

Brick spit into his hand and told Ray to bend over the
chair. Ray loved the feeling of being like this. Strange
that being so vulnerable and so open could make him feel
so safe. Trust was not something he felt often in the world,
but he felt it consistently with Brick.

Ray felt Brick's lips on his backside. Those familiar kisses never grew tiresome. Licking so gently there. Ray started to squirm and move his hips. Pushing back onto Brick's tongue. He felt so right being penetrated this way. A delicious intrusion that was only making way for much more to come. Ray reached back and pulled Brick's head closer. "I need you."

Brick lifted his head, "Now?"

"Now."

Brick stood and spit on his member. He advanced slowly. A gradual teasing. "Feel good?"

"Amazing." Ray contracted tighter. Wanting to feel more and simultaneously wanting it to last forever. He couldn't have both, but anymore had no idea what was possible. So many things were happening that he never could have imagined. Ray turned his head to look at Brick, "God, I love you."

Brick reached around. Ray's penis was already flush to his belly.

Ray rose and reached back. Hands on Brick's hips. Pulling Brick closer. Pulling him deeper. This wonderful feeling always made him want more. Maybe Ray was that way with a lot of things, like stardom, like booze.

Brick was moving faster. As if by instinct, Brick knew when to take control and when to lose it completely. The time was right.

"Do it."

"I'm there. I..."

Ray turned his head and rose to kiss him. The contortion was worth any risk of strain. "I love you."

"Love you too, baby. You'll be terrific tomorrow."

Ray looked him in the eyes. "Whatever happens at the reading tomorrow is small potatoes, being with you is what really matters."

26

Ray felt a a shiver run through his spine as he was ushered through the front gates of Triumph Pictures. He half expected the guards to give him the bum's rush. Triumph was on a par with Metropolitan. Success in this picture for this studio would mean big things. He'd studied the part. He knew the lines. He understood the emotional arc. Preparation was done. All that remained was the doing.

On his way to the office, he bumped into several people who he used to know. One stepped up and shook his hand. Ray couldn't remember the player's name—the worst affront to an actor. When he found out Ray was auditioning, he wished him luck. The other pretended she didn't see him. Ray was sure he had offended her at some time. He could do nothing to change the past. Ray could only work to change his behavior in the future.

The studio secretary was polished and efficient. Ray was happy she recognized him, and he didn't have to introduce himself. "Right this way, Mr. Richmond." On the flip side, he was sometimes recognized as "that jerk" or "that drunk" or "that pansy." But folks in this town only saw you that way when you were down and out.

She ushered Ray into a large room. The camera was set. Ray hadn't realized the audition was going to be filmed. Already standing in the room were a cameraman, a director, and an offscreen actress to feed him lines. They all introduced themselves, but Ray was so nervous he forgot their names in two shakes. The last two people in the room were Genevieve and Lucas. They were in charge of evaluating his performance. With the exception of director approval by Victor Petrovich and star approval from Kay Francis, Genevieve and Lucas were powers that be in casting his role in *Beyond the Pale*.

His role? The role.

He was Test #6. Five others had auditioned for the part already, and more would follow.

Genevieve asked if he was ready.

"As ready as I'll ever be." He was set. Terrified, but set. He slowed his breathing to try and focus.

The director called for action. The actress cued his speech. And Ray delivered. He felt himself vanish. Memorization gave way to spontaneous feeling. The lines went from being the work of a screenwriter to being the genuine words of his character. Ray lost himself in the role and, for a few moments, he became Eddie. When he finished, it was like waking from a dream. Disoriented. His heart pounded. He felt tears in his eyes. Had he cried during his line delivery? He was unsure if he'd been terrific or horrible, only that the audition had happened. Despite all his experience, acting had never felt so genuine.

Everyone in the room was silent.

Ray wondered if that was good.

A moment later, people actually applauded. *No one ever applauded during auditions.*

Genevieve and Lucas told him he was terrific. Ray wanted to believe them, but he'd been in Hollywood a long time. People didn't typically give it to you straight. They went on, saying they were thrilled with his interpretation of Eddie. This was too excessive for empty flattery. "You brought so much more to the role than what is just in the script," added Genevieve.

"It was a privilege hearing that," said Lucas. "You will definitely be hearing from us, Raymond. Probably next week. We'll still need to show the screen test to Petrovich and some of the studio executives."

"I understand. And thanks for the chance."

Lucas put a hand on Ray's shoulder. "We all deserve a chance, governor." Lucas said, somehow forming the words around the cigarette dangling from his mouth. "So good to have you back. We have a few more people to see."

Ray thanked the small crew for helping with the audition. The director and the cameraman shook his hand and wished him luck. The line actress gave him a hug and whispered to him that she had a Raymond Richmond scrapbook as a teen. "Meeting you was a dream come true."

Ray had a good feeling about today, but sometimes the good feelings were as frightening as the bad ones. Good feelings brought expectations and having expectations came with the possibility of such disappointment.

That evening Brick came home from some sound consultation at First National. He was carrying a bouquet and handed Ray the flowers.

Ray laughed. "Remember when you nabbed flowers?"

Brick shook his head and smiled. "Took me a bit to realize Hollywood isn't Montana and you couldn't just go and pick them."

Ray was on cloud nine. "You should have seen me today. I did good, at least I think I did."

"Yes, you did." Brick said he had talked to Genevieve.

Ray wanted to know everything she said. Brick slipped off his shoes and explained there wasn't much to tell. "Only that you were sensational and everyone in the room was very impressed. They talked about you the rest of the day."

Ray lifted Brick's feet to his lap and began to massage them. He bent down and took Brick's big toe in his mouth. He pulled it out with a pop, and smiled. "Whatever happens from here on out, I know it has nothing to do with my abilities. Today, for the first time, I felt like a terrific actor. Not a movie star, but an actor. And I owe it all to you."

"That is a gift you were born with, pure and simple. You owe me nothing. Your happiness is enough."

"Maybe for now," replied Ray, taking two toes in his mouth. He took them out and licked up the side of Brick's foot before returning to his toes. "You like that?"

Brick groped his crotch and grinned. "You need to ask?"

"Tell me."

"I like that."

"What do you like?"

"I like having you suck my toes."

Ray put both of Brick's big toes in his mouth, but then stopped. "What's wrong with you, you seem a thousand miles away."

Brick pulled his feet down and yawned. "I'm sorry. Guess I'm just tired."

"Really?"

Brick reached out and took his hand. "Really."

***

Brick couldn't block this anxiety or silence the voices in his head. Ray's audition had been terrific. That should make him happy, but Ray had thrown Brick over for his career before. Once he started to fret about Ray leaving him, it was impossible to shake the thought. Brick wondered if he was a fool for trusting his heart to Ray a second time. The problem was, he had no choice, Ray had been in possession of his heart since the day they met. What Brick really feared was losing this happiness. He had survived without it for years, and then the joy had returned. He was unsure if he could endure losing it again.

Sleep usually stopped his doom scenarios. Cleared his head. That night sleep eluded him. Brick lay awake. He worried this idyllic life they built had a foundation of sand, that it all could be swept away in a moment. He left the bed and moved to the patio. The nighttime chill felt refreshing.

Ray joined him moments later. "I heard you get up. Is everything okay?"

"Fine. Just can't sleep."

Ray leaned over the chair and enveloped Brick in his arms. "You always feel so good."

Brick smiled.

"I worried you were sick. Don't stay out here too late." He gave Brick a deep kiss. "Love you."

Brick pulled Ray's arms tighter about him. "Love you, too. I always will."

Ray padded back into the bungalow.

***

Ray stretched awake and reached out to find an empty place beside him on the mattress. He remembered Brick in the garden. He had been behaving so strangely. He was so distant last night. Had he stayed up all night? Ray walked into the living room. Brick was stretched out on the couch with those long legs off the side of the sofa and on the floor. He was dead to the world. The morning was chilly. Ray took an afghan and draped it over him. He wondered why Brick was sleeping out here. Ray wondered if he was mad. *Have I done something?* Since they'd come back together, they'd never been apart. He hoped everything was okay.

Ray tried to be quiet as he made coffee and fed Amelia and Sophie. Amelia wasn't quite so concerned. When she heard her food being prepared leapt from the back of the couch directly onto Brick's stomach before jumping down to the floor and running over to the kitchen.

Brick awoke with a sputter.

"I was trying to be quiet," winced Ray.

Brick rolled on his side. He still looked half asleep. "Amelia finds perverse joy in doing things like that," he croaked.

They laughed and things seemed suddenly back to normal.

Ray wondered if he was making something out of nothing. Sharing a small amusing moment felt good.

27

In the following days, Ray tried to keep himself occupied
with the same things he had been busy with before the big
audition. In the mornings, he walked across the courtyard
and picked up Todd, and they took the bus to whatever
studio was on the slate for the day. Before, Todd had been
the one leading the way. Now, Ray determined where they
would go. He usually had something slated. He tried to get
Todd work whenever he could.

Things were getting easier for Ray. Much of his old
confidence had returned, but he was cautious and
remained vigilant that it didn't cross over into conceit. An
inflated ego had meant disaster before. Besides, if his fall
had taught him anything, it was that he could count on

nothing in this business. He'd heard far too many promises in Hollywood to give any of them much weight.

While waiting for word on *Beyond the Pale*, he was cast for two days work in a George Raft picture. He was pleased to get the part and to be promised billing in the opening credits, even though he was listed tenth. He talked the casting people into giving Todd a recurring part as a drunk in the nightclub scenes.

Todd was beside himself. "They said they were going to give me a couple close-ups and do a long shot on my wobble-leg walk. That's one of my signature gags."

Ray agreed that was terrific. Before all this had happened, he never realized how nice it was to do favors for others and expect nothing in return. He never knew how good it felt to simply be kind. The ecstatic look on Todd's face gave Ray such a feeling of warmth inside. That response was his victory as well. Todd's smile proved to Ray that he had changed. He was being regular. Despite all the rotten things he had done, he had just made that guy's day.

On the bus ride home, Todd amused their fellow riders by testing out the different sort of drunk antics he was going to use in the film.

"Save some of it for the cameras," Ray finally said.

"Don't worry about that. When it comes to gags, I'm like Old Faithful. I never run dry. There's plenty more where this came from."

Ray laughed. "At this rate people are going to leave that theater saying, *Was George Raft even in that picture?*"

As scheduled, Ray and Todd wrapped their work on the George Raft picture in two days. The shoot went well. Glenda Farrell told Todd she was going to request him for her next picture. "There aren't enough great clowns around anymore," she had said.
Todd talked about their conversation on the entire bus ride home the second day. Ray hoped she followed through on her promise. He didn't like the thought of Todd being disappointed.

"The guy deserves a break," he said to Brick that night.

Brick agreed. "Nobody works harder in this town, that's for sure."

Ray saw the paint on Brick's dungarees. "You working on anything."

"Just dabbling."

"Can I see?"

"I'll show you when I'm done." Brick was eager to change the subject. "Dinner is on the stove and should be ready in about a half hour. Now, what can we do until then?" Brick pulled Ray down on the couch. "Maybe we could have a little appetizer." Ray could feel his urgency as Brick kissed his neck. He loved that all the strangeness that had surrounded Brick the past few days seemed to be gone. He loved that Brick couldn't keep his hands off him.

"Meat as the first course isn't customary, but..." Ray reached down and unbuttoned Brick's fly. Rigid. Ready. Ray gripped him. Stroked his firmness. Brick slapped him on the ass a couple of times. On the third stroke, he rubbed Ray's bum through his trousers. Ray kissed his way down Brick's torso. Lower until he reached the prize. Coursing its surface with his tongue. Pulling it from Brick's belly. Poised before taking it whole. Swallowing. Such a perfect man smell. Brick grabbing his hair. Ray wanting more, more than every bit of him. Balls. Pungent. A day's work. Musky smell. The scent made Ray crazed. Sucking again. Harder. Mouth taking no prisoners. Hand clamped at the base, the other rising in tandem.

"Damn."

Ray began to hum. A slight vibration. Another trick to enhance the perfect pleasure. Brick pulling his hair now. Breathing harder. Hips rising off the couch. Wouldn't be long.

"God. Yes."

Brick slipped a hand his below the band of Ray's boxers. His index finger teased, hitting the mark and causing a gasp. Brick retrieved the digit. A whiff of Ray. His fingers returned, this time coated in saliva. Brick slipped the tip of a digit inside. To the knuckle. Curling to touch the nut of Ray'a prostate.

Ray shook but was undeterred. His sucking continued with a fervor.

Brick retrieved his fingers. Coating a second in spit. Soon Ray was riding two digits. Hard to focus on his sucking and Brick's cock with so much in and out. Brick yanked Ray's pants to his ankles.

"Squat above my face," Brick ordered.

Ray obeyed, spreading his cheeks above Brick as he reclined on the couch, and then descending. Brick strained to make contact before pulling Ray down by the hips. Harder. Nibbling between nuts and hole. That drove Ray wild. Always had.

"Fuck me!"

"You ready? You ready to get fucked?"

They stood and Brick bent him over the couch.

Ray wanted it so badly. He wanted to be wrecked and saved. Beaten and blessed. He needed Brick to shatter the ache of need. "Fuck me," he cried over his shoulder, turning to see Brick positioning himself. Brick said he'd give it slow. Ray said fast. Brick entered and Ray moved back hard, driving Brick deep inside. Ray tensed, clamping, controlling. Using his muscles to milk Brick's manhood. He tightened even more as Brick withdrew to the crown. Ray smiled to feel him shudder. Both could give as good as they took. Brick began to slam. To the base. Faster and deeper and upping the pace. His hands were wrapped over Ray's shoulders. His lips were at the nape of Ray's neck. Faster. Full force. Both men were slick with sweat. Droplets fell from Brick's hair onto Ray's back,.

"You feel so good."

Ray felt the world expanding along with Brick. The pulse of the universe that joined them. The big man shook. Ray knew and reached down. He was only one stroke behind. Ready now at any time. Then the time was now. And it was happening. Exploding from Ray and exploding inside of him.The two men's cries blended. Spasms rocked the two as one, the single being which desire had created.

After the pulse of the moment had ebbed, Brick eased onto his back. "Whew," he said. "That just keeps getting better."

"Agreed." Ray kissed him. "I love when you're an animal just as much as when you are a man."

Brick got up from the couch and put the dinner on a lower flame. "There, now we'll have time for a shower."

28

A few days later, Ray was home on the couch petting Amelia when the telephone rang. The casting office was on the line. Ray felt his pulse race.

"Raymond, this is Genevieve Gaines. We met when you auditioned for *Beyond the Pale*."

"Yes, nice to hear from you." Of course he remembered.

"We need you to take a meeting with Kay Francis and the film's director, Victor Petrovich, this Wednesday. Would that be convenient?"

Ray said yes. He'd make sure it was convenient.

"Perfect. I will pass on word and someone will call you with the details."

"Thank you. Thank you so much."

He could hear the smile in Genevieve's voice. "You're welcome. But this is just a second meeting."

"I know, but thank you."

"Someone will call about Wednesday."

Ray suspected this meeting was some sort of test and if all went well, the part would be his. At least that was what he hoped. His mind changed scenarios a dozen times in the next hour alone. He'd just have to wait and see.

He told Brick the minute he walked through the door. "What do you think it means?"

"Well, they wouldn't be meeting with you to let you know you didn't get the part. That would be a phone call, if you were lucky. The studio is just not that considerate. Remember, this is Hollywood."

Ray laughed. "That is something I find impossible to forget."

Brick sat beside him on the couch. "And Genevieve would never call personally."

"Not even if she was a friend of yours?"

Brick put an arm around him. "Not even." Brick kissed him on the cheek. "I'd say the best way to look at Wednesday is just to consider it another sort of audition. But I'd take odds that it's a very positive thing."

Ray tried to relax. He tried to think of this lunch as a social get together, and not a confirmation of his getting the role. That would make the disappointment easier just in case. He had technically met Kay years ago at someone's party. They had gotten along together quite well, at least Ray thought so. Maybe that had been someone else. *No*, Ray thought shaking his head. *That was Kay Francis.*

At the time, Kay Francis had been a young starlet. Ray was the big star. Kay was fresh off the train from New York. She was tall, sleek and gorgeous, with lovely almond shaped eyes. Even then, rumors circulated that the elegant ingenue preferred the company of ladies to men and that she was part of Hollywood's "sewing circle" of women who loved women. The ladies were much smarter about those things. They tended to keep things behind closed doors. They practiced discretion. Their scandals were whispered. Ray's exploits had often involved outsiders and coppers and eventually the tabloids.

Ray hoped he'd been kind to Kay when they met. If not, he hoped she was forgiving. So often his behavior from those years was a blur. He had some idea as to who he had insulted and who he hadn't, but he often offended even those he didn't directly insult.

***

After Ray told him about the lunch, Brick had called Victor Petrovich. Brick was thrilled that Victor was directing *Beyond the Pale*. Victor was a terrific director, and he also owed Brick a big favor. Brick had done some last minute sound work for him a couple years back. Brick wasn't going to tell Ray about their connection. That would only cause Ray to doubt his talents or overestimate his chances.

"Victor, how have you been?"

"Wonderful."

Brick toyed with the cord. He knew Victor was a busy man and didn't know how to broach the subject. "I'm not sure if you are aware, but my roommate is Raymond Richmond."

"Yes, I knew."

"Well, I..."

Victor didn't allow him to finish. "Brick, it is a joy to hear from you, but you needn't have called." Victor explained he was already keen on casting Raymond. Mainly he and Kay and the executives wanted to be sure Raymond arrived on time, and that he showed up sober, and lacking a star attitude. "I have a picture to make. I don't have time for a drunk or a big ego. Neither will Kay."

"He's reformed. A different man. He really is," offered Brick.

There was a long pause in the conversation before Victor resumed, "So Brick, you are the mystery man to thank for Raymond's turn around?"

"He turned his own life around. All I did was believe in him."

Victor assured him that sometimes that was the greatest gift one can give another, "Especially when that person is an artist. People of that temperament are often plagued with doubts. How long have you know him?"

"I've known him for years, but he moved in here with me a few months ago."

Victor said he couldn't be happier for him, and for both of them. "Love is very hard to find. Be sure you never lose it. I would not still be walking this earth if it weren't for my Elena."

29

The following day, Ray arrived sober and on time for the lunch meeting at the studio commissary. He saw Victor a moment later. The director approached him. "So nice to meet you, Mr. Richmond."

"Nice to meet you, Mr. Petrovich. Call me Ray. I am a big admirer of your work."

Victor thanked him. "And please, call me Victor. And I am an admirer of your films as well."

Despite the inflated ego he used to display, Ray was awkward about accepting direct praise. He blushed. "Well, I'm hoping *Beyond the Pale* will be the start of a new phase in my career."

"I am hopeful as well."

Victor said he felt *Beyond the Pale* would be a very important picture.

Ray was in enthusiastic agreement. "It confronts a lot of things about war that pictures don't show."

"Until now." Victor added.

The men were so involved in the discussion that neither saw Kay approach. When she arrived at their table, both men stood. Ray got her chair. Kay offered a hand. "Don't let me put a cork in your conversation. I'm in wholehearted agreement. I think this picture will be one we can all be proud of."

All three raised their water glasses in a toast to the upcoming picture. Ray didn't want to take anything for granted, but given the direction and the inclusive nature of the conversation, he wondered if he had the role. Victor and Ms. Francis wouldn't use the word "we" if he wasn't being offered the part. Would they?

Kay said she was eager for an acting stretch after her ongoing string of weepy dramas. "This one will be a weeper as well, but one with some meat on it's bones. Isn't that right, Victor?"

Victor said if God was willing.

"This one wouldn't steer me wrong," Kay nodded towards the director. "He'd better not anyway or I'll clobber him," she added. Kay lit her next cigarette before putting out her current gasper. "I adore my fans and am grateful for my success, but sometimes as an artist, there's an itch for more, to challenge yourself and keep it all interesting." Kay took a gander at the clock and focussed on the avocado salad which appeared at her place the moment she arrived at the table. Ray watched her closely. Such class. Innate sophistication. No one could debate that, at least in public, Kay Francis was ever the cultured and impeccably put-together star. She'd topped Hollywood's best dressed list for several years running and there were no challengers to the crown in the offing. She turned to Ray. "We've met before, you know."

The blood rushed from Ray's face.

Kay laughed. "Oh my. Don't worry. Aside from being soused, you were fairly harmless."

"Well, that's behind me now."

"Good. Because I don't want that hindering the picture. You understand."

Ray swallowed. She was being a good egg. Straightforward. Fair. Kind. Regular. "I completely understand."

"Good. That's all I really had to say."

After a few more minutes, Victor asked for the tab and signed his name. Kay kissed both men on the cheek and said she had to dash. "I'm posing for stills this afternoon," she said with a quick check of her make-up. "I don't know why I bother. They just redo everything the moment I get back in front of the cameras."

As they left the commissary, Victor turned to Ray and said he had something for him. He ankled over to fetch a leather folder from the passenger seat of his breezer, the full script of *Beyond the Pale*. "Congratulations. Kay and I are on board. The part of Eddie is yours. We begin shooting next week. I'll have a messenger deliver call times and details."

Ray was beside himself. "Oh my God, thank you for this, Mr. Petrovich." Ray held the script to his chest. "I promise you won't regret it."

"Victor," he corrected.

"Thank you, Victor. I won't let you down."

"I think you will be wonderful in the part. I have every confidence in you."

When Brick arrived home at the end of his day, Ray took him in his arms and spun him around the bungalow floor. He was nodding. "Uh huh. Uh huh. I got it. I got it. I got the part. I am going to be Eddie."

Brick kissed him. "You'll be a perfect Eddie."

Amelia hopped off the couch. The excited terrier barked at their feet as they moved about the floor. Sophie watched with disdain from a bookshelf before turning away. Ray was kissing Brick. "I got it. I actually got it. The part is mine. We start shooting next week."

"Wow, that's fast."

"Kay has a pretty full schedule. We have just enough time to shoot it before she starts her next weeper."

"I'm so thrilled or you. I'm prouder than any man has a right to be."

Ray felt such gratitude. "I owe it all to you."

Brick shook his head. "Not me. Us. This," he added gesturing to the both of them. "The combo of you and me is what makes us great. Together we can do anything. This is only the beginning."

Ray wondered what he meant. *The beginning*. His imagination began to run rampant. He tried to keep it in check. He didn't need to muse on things down the road and future successes. Something terrific was happening right now, and he didn't want to miss a moment of it.

Two days later Ray went in for fittings. Wardrobe took hours but everyone seemed pleased. Tuxedo, riding clothes, doughboy uniform. Despite hard living, Ray still cut a dashing figure. His waistline had not varied an inch since his prime. Next came make-up. Blessed with photogenic features and fine bone structure, Ray didn't need too much in that department.

When Ray got home that evening, he was exhausted. Brick should have been home hours ago. The bungalow was dark. When he stepped inside he saw the candles. "Happy Birthday, Baby."

Ray couldn't believe he'd forgotten his thirtieth birthday, then he remembered it was tomorrow. He didn't want to spoil the moment by saying he had the wrong day. Ray was beside himself. Brick and a cake and the animals. Though it was just them in the bungalow, no birthday ever seemed grander. "I can't believe you remembered or even knew."

"I have my ways."

"Oh, mysterious. And what are the rest of your powers."

"Wouldn't you like to know."

Ray said he would.

Brick dropped to his knees in reply. He fumbled with the buttons of Ray's pants. A moment later he slid his slacks to his knees. Brick reached inside. "I've always wanted to make it with a movie star."

Ray laughed.

Afterwards, the men lay naked on the couch. Ray took his hand and kissed his palm, "I didn't want to say anything earlier and ruin the party, but my birthday is tomorrow."

Brick kissed him. "I know. Just wanted to make sure that your twenties ended properly. What until you see what I do at the start of a decade."

"You're crazy."

Brick kissed him tenderly and looked deep into his eyes. "You make me that way. I'm crazy for you, my love and because of that, I've never felt saner."

30

The remainder of the week passed in a blur of fittings and rewrites and rehearsals. This was the sort of hectic Ray enjoyed. He felt he was doing something important, involved in life again aside from his relationship with Brick.

As an actor, it was so nice to be in an A picture. A pictures had rehearsal time and takes and continuity and sound and camera precision that cut the mustard when it came to the finished product. By the following Monday when Ray walked onto the set for the first day of shooting, he walked in Eddie's shoes. He'd never been so ready for anything. Certainly nothing in his film career. In his previous movies, everything was so rushed to keep his films in the theaters, Ray didn't have time to prepare much less appreciate the process. He'd never felt a character like he did with Eddie. Despite being a top notch production, *Beyond the Pale* was a quick shoot requiring three full weeks. Ray would have his scenes shot and in the can by the end of the week. Ray had no problem with the quick shooting schedule. He was known as a first or second take actor.

The first set-up Ray shot was one of the early scenes of his character, before Eddie goes to war. Ray, as Eddie, was supposed to run into a room full of revelers and shout, "To blazes with the neighbors, we're dancing until dawn." When Petrovich called action, Ray waited for his cue and came running through the door, but instead of delivering his line, he slipped on the polished tile and went pinwheeling across the room before falling. When he got up, the gathered cast and crew were laughing. The old Ray would have been furious. Instead, Ray joined in their laughter. He took a deep bow.

"Would you mind doing that again, the focus was off." Kay joked.

His unintentional mishap cut the first day tension on the set. The second time he came through the door, he did it perfectly. Hitting his mark and saying the line just right. Petrovich nodded. Ray could tell he was pleased.

The week was unlike any Ray had experienced as an actor. When the lights were set, and he was in costume with the cameras were ready to roll, Ray went into character. He could lose himself in the role of Eddie as he'd never done with a part before, delivering his lines and understanding why they were said. Cast and crew, and most importantly Ray, knew he was giving the performance of his career.

Something had changed in his approach to acting. Awareness. Compassion, Understanding. He felt grounded, and his character had also acquired a gravity that reflected his work. Ray's view of everything had deepened with his sobriety and his relationship with Brick. As a result ,Ray had a new respect for his craft, and an appreciation for the medium he never had before. A lifetime ago, he'd been a movie star and a matinee idol. He'd been blind to so much of life, and he was sure that hollowness had translated into his performances. Now after so many years in the business, Ray felt he had finally become an actor. And a damn good one.

When Victor reviewed the *Beyond the Pale* rushes at the end of the week, he made a point of taking Ray aside and telling him his performance was superb. "Your part is key in the transformation of Kay from socialite to a woman of substance. Her change hinges on the Eddie role, and you make us believe it. You hit the bullseye with Eddie."

Ray was beside himself. "Thank you so much for the opportunity."

"Thank you for rising to meet the challenge. I don't wish to swell your head or anything, but your work in this film could win you some awards, my friend. Not that I put much stock in those things." Victor said he was going to talk to the boys in the main office and see what they had to say about extending his contract for a few more pictures. "After seeing your work in *Beyond the Pale*, they are bound to realize keeping you at the studio is in their best interests."

"Victor, I'd really appreciate it. That would be wonderful." Ray was beyond delighted. He didn't know what to say. He felt tears begin to well in his eyes.

Victor put a hand on his shoulder.

"I'm so grateful. I never thought I'd be... I've waited so long for this moment, this vindication and it has just hit me in a way I didn't expect. I thought I'd messed up any chance I had of returning."

"Think again. You're back."

"I'm back," Ray said softly to himself.

When he got home that evening, Brick was painting in the garden. Ray told him the good news. Brick said he knew he would hit the jackpot. He said he'd known all along.

"I know you did. Your faith saved me. You believed in me when I'd lost all hope in myself."

Brick kissed him. "Thank you. But don't put me on some sort of pedestal. I'm just a man in love."

The two were locked in a kiss and undoing buttons when Ray heard a knock on the door.

"Anybody home?" It was Todd.

With his eyes locked on Ray, Brick called. "Be there in just a minute." They quickly buttoned their trousers.

Todd was excited about getting another two day role. This time he was playing a frustrated cook in a ZaSu Pitts picture. "I toss pizzas and wear the big chef hat, the whole bit. Lots of slapstick fodder right there. The producers are very keen on me. Have been from the get go. I wouldn't be surprised if Glenda put in a good word for me. She said she was going to."

"Congratulations. ZaSu is a doll," offered Ray.

"I haven't worked with her in years. Since some atrocious backlot picture with John Bunny that hopefully never saw the light of day. I doubt she'll even remember me."

Todd turned to Ray. "Now for the real reason I came by. So, tell me, how did it go?"

"What?"

Todd gave an exaggerated eye-roll. "What do you think? The final day of the *Beyond the Pale* shoot." Todd confessed that he had wanted to run over to the bungalow every evening to ask how filming was going, but didn't know if Ray was superstitious about such things. Many actors didn't like to discuss a part when they were in the middle of a shoot.

"It went really well."

"Yeah?"

Ray lit a cigarette. "Really well. Rumor is they're going to offer me a contract at Triumph Pictures."

"This calls for a celebration." Todd looked at Ray and then Brick and noticed Ray's untucked shirt. He realized that his knock had interrupted the celebration. "Jeepers. I'm sorry. I didn't realize that you two were making whoopie. I feel like a real fire extinguisher."

"It's okay." Ray and Brick were laughing.

"I'm only going to stay a minute."

Ray told him to stay as long as he liked.

"Within reason," joked Brick.

"As you were saying," said Ray with a roll of his eyes.

"Ray, I am so thrilled. A contract? So it is possible. There is indeed life after studio death. Let me stand close to you. Maybe some of that magic dust will rub off onto me."

Brick offered him some iced tea. "Sounds like things are going good for you as well. After all, you came in here crowing the news about your two day role."

Todd shrugged. "That's a long way from a contract, but things are going much better than they were."

Ray and Brick reassured Todd some great vehicle would be coming down the pipeline so on.

"Long as they don't want me to talk." Todd's career was stronger than it had been in several years, but he was also no dumbbell. He'd told Ray countless times that he knew he came across a little too fey on film. "I'm too much a three-letter man for mid-America." Even back in vaudeville, he said he was getting laughs for just being who he was. At the time, he figured he might as well get paid for it. He'd said to Ray that the silents were a godsend. "Entertaining without speaking was a dream come true. That dream ended with the advent of sound." Todd's talkie career was improving, but he confessed it would never be like before. Audiences were gaga over voices.

After finishing his lemonade, Todd said he had to get going. "I'll leave you two to it."

Brick blushed.

"Don't do anything I wouldn't do without throwing out my back." Todd called as the screen door closed.

Brick turned to Ray. "Hope he'll be all right."

"He'll be fine. He loves this business. He knows as well as anyone how fickle it can be. One day people want you, the next you're old hat. He's also been around long enough to know that stardom has little to do with talent."

"You're right."

"Am I?" Ray kissed him deeply.

"So right."

Ray was extremely blessed to have Brick. To have what they had. The passion. The admiration. Support. A love that had saved his life. That had transformed him. Ray liked who he had become and who he was with Brick. What they had was real. Sometimes he was so terrified this dream, this everyday miracle, was going to end.

Brick dove on top of him. "You're thinking too much." Brick began kissing his neck. Tongue wiggling in his ear.

"That tickles. Stop."

"Only if you stop thinking... and get rid of the clothes."

Ray loved when Brick was eager for him. *Relentless. Ravenous.* Sex helped dispel his insecurity. Brick's desire for him proved everything between them was solid. It proved everything would endure. Wouldn't it? Ray arched his back as Brick took him in his mouth. So good. Another perfect moment. Ray wanted to believe in forever, but he knew the future held no guarantees. Life could be even more unpredictable than Hollywood.

31

The following week, Ray got a phone call from a secretary at Triumph. Red Scarno, the head of Triumph Pictures, wanted to see him. "Mr. Scarno requests you to be at his office tomorrow at two."

Ray knew the appointment time was not optional. The appointment had already been entered in ink. Scarno's meeting time was an edict if Ray wanted to sign with Triumph Pictures. No one said no to Red Scarno. Ray affirmed that he would be there at two. The secretary said she would see him then.

Ray hung up the phone. This was it. He was being ushered back into the fold. The next phase of his return was in motion. He went out to the patio and sat for a while. The sunshine felt so good. Amelia jumped up on his lap. Sophie perched nearby, cleaning herself. Ray felt at peace here, just petting the dog and doing nothing. He'd never appreciated contentment before. He'd considered it a bad thing, one step away from the grave. Contentment was a deterrent to being driven, to achieving success.

He walked over to the easel. Curious to see what Brick had been working on, he lifted the cloth. Oils. The painting was only about halfway finished. A subject in skin tones—he and Brick, naked, in one another arms. Just after. *Beautiful. Sensual.* The canvas left little to the imagination. A study in detail as well as emotion, Brick's love came through with every brushstroke. The painting was accurate except for Brick's scar. He returned the cover cloth. Brick would unveil the piece when he was ready.

The next day. Ray arrived at Triumph promptly at the appointed time. He took a seat in the outer office. Evelyn, the secretary, asked if he would like something to drink.

"Just water would be fine."

Scarno kept him waiting until ten after. Ray expected something like that. *Intimidation*. All the big boys played the same game. Ray knew all the power ploys of studio executives. They didn't get to where they were by being on equal footing with the talent.

Ray entered Scarno's office and looked around. Everything was oversized. A huge desk that sat on a pedestal ran along the back wall of the room. Behind it, windows twenty feet high were adorned with rich brocaded curtains. Two men stood at either side of the desk. A couple of baby grands. Scarno was between them, on the phone with his back to Ray. "Well get it in on time. I don't care. I don't care. Don't come to me with problems, come to me with solutions. Yes. Solve it or I'll find someone who can." He hung up the phone without another word. Turning, he stood and walked around the desk to shake Ray's hand. "Raymond Richmond. I thought you were dead."

Ray ignored the comment. "Mr. Scarno, pleased to meet you."

"I've been hearing terrific things about you from Victor and Kay. They are predicting all sorts of accolades for *Beyond the Pale*."

Ray tried to remain humble. "Well, I had a terrific director, and Miss Francis is a very gracious star."

Scarno pulled a cigar from the case on the corner of his desk. One of the assistants leapt to give him fire. With a deep puff, Scarno moved back behind his desk. "Let me cut to the chase and tell you why I brought you here. I'd like to put you under contract with Triumph."

Ray felt the fluttering in his chest. The moment he'd been waiting for had arrived. Without a studio behind you, you're no one in Hollywood. "I'm flattered."

"You should be. I don't do this every day. Especially not with someone with your history. I'm willing to forget all that." Scarno explained that he was eager to sign Ray for a three year contract which stipulated both starring and supporting roles. "You are a double threat. I think you can carry a B picture and that you'll succeed as a character actor in A features. More than just a pretty face. You've developed the acting chops to go along with it." The beefy assistants to his left and to his right nodded.

Ray tried to remain calm. Raymond Richmond had once more become a hot commodity. Scarno was willing to forget his past and sign him to a new three-year contract with options. The pay was not as lofty as it once was, but it was well beyond anything Ray thought he would ever see again.

This was all really happening.

Scarno explained that even though Ray had become a hot property once again, the studio had some concerns and conditions. "I won't put up with the nonsense Metropolitan tolerated. I don't need to."

Ray knew what he was talking about. His throat tightened at the mention of conditions. He clenched his hands. Scarno offered a smoke from the ivory case on his desk. A gasper would help about now. Give him time to think. *Inhale. Exhale. Inhale…* At Scarno's nod, an assistant lit it for him.

Scarno leaned back in his chair and blew a perfect smoke ring from his cigar. "Now Raymond, these conditions have little effect on your professional life and film choices. However, we have some stipulations regarding our player's personal lives. A morals clause is common these days, but we feel we need to be a bit more specific given your particular circumstances."

Ray nodded.

"Given your past conduct in the public eye and the amount we're willing to invest in your career, we have some reservations. We need some guarantees. We'll ignore your past mistakes, but you need to change your image."

Ray took a deep drag of his cigarette and tried to keep his face impassive.

"We're eager for you begin dating Lorna Chandler, one of our top starlets. That should put the rumors about your more unseemly activities to rest. In a few months, you two can wed. I see a full magazine spread for the vows. Lorna is very amicable to the arrangement and is willing to make no personal demands on you. I see a child when the timing is right. The union will be of great advantage to both your careers. The publicity department will be working overtime."

Ray said he couldn't marry Lorna for obvious reasons. Ray also explained he was in a relationship.

"Yeah, yeah. I know all about it. Brick is a terrific guy, but a nobody. A behind the scenes guy. No one will notice. Of course it goes without saying that you can never be seen with that fairy in public and you'll need to vacate his residence as soon as possible."

Ray felt his hands begin to shake.

Scarno pointed out the window of his office. "Personally, I don't agree with that sort of thing, but mostly I don't give a damn. It's the audiences we have to convince. The people in Topeka need to see you as a red blooded American male. So that's what we'll give them. You're wise to the workings of this town. That life you have with Brick can continue, but very discreetly, and certainly not in the public eye." Scarno put the contract down in front of Ray and handed him a pen.

Ray took a deep breath. Ink glistened at the tip of the pen. Everything he'd been praying for was right there for the taking. Easy as signing his name.

Scarno bridged his fingers in front of his mouth. "Raymond, regarding your work schedule. We are looking at four or five pictures per year with one-time refusal rights during that period. That's the best deal to be had in this town. You ought to be grateful. Second chances don't come around that often, especially ones this good."

"You're right, they don't." Ray was overwhelmed by the six page document, the details of everything being offered, and all that was being asked of him as well. He somewhat knew what to expect. He hadn't anticipated the conditions being so firm when it came to Brick. *Move out?* Ray loved it there. *Paradise.* But the movies were his home as well. The decision was not an easy one. Ray snubbed out his smoke and stood. He folded the contract. He told Scarno he needed to think about it.

Scarno gripped his hand in a tight handshake and held it a bit longer than necessary. "I hope you're just overwhelmed. Don't *think* about signing for too long. I don't take kindly to ingratitude."

Ray accurately gauged the threat in Scarno's words. Even if Ray signed eventually, the fact he had not done so immediately meant that his relationship with Scarno would start out strained. Ray had mostly forgotten about the Hollywood games and the egos. *The politics. The bullshit.* Constant worries about being in so and so's good graces.

On the drive home, Ray had the cab driver stop at a little roadside place, a gin mill. A belt sounded good. He did it without even thinking. He needed something to clear his head and quiet his mind. This Triumph decision was important. He needed to weigh his options. He'd worked hard to get back on his feet, but he realized today the first step in his comeback was to betray the person he loved most in the world.

"To new beginnings," he toasted himself in the mirror. He took a swig from his glass. The warmth spread through him almost immediately. He looked around. The tavern was dark but the shadows were familiar. A stuffed polar bear stood in the corner near the restrooms. Ray remembered.

The last time he'd been here, it was a speakeasy. He'd still been under contract at Metropolitan across town. Ray had been downing rotgut that night. Plenty of it. The home still stuff really had a kick to it. *One for the road. Two for the road. Another round.* Someone from the studio eventually came to get him after a tip off that he was there. By the time the rep had arrived, he was a complete mess. The studio runner hustled him out the back door with a coat over his head in case photographers were waiting, and then poured him into the waiting car.

Ray closed his eyes. He shook his head to recall the drunken pass he'd then made at the studio assistant. A hand on the knee and an invitation to swim in his pool. *Lecherous lush.* So ashamed. Here he was again. Same place. He was back all right, in more ways than one. He eyed the glass. Not even an hour and already he was moving down that same road. He pushed his drink away. In the mirror behind the bar, he saw the desperation on his face. What the hell was he doing? Ray rose from his stool. Scarno was right. Second chances don't come around too often.

Ray went out into sunlight and began walking. He'd been holding his breath. The afternoon air felt good. This would clear his mind more than a drink. Ray recalled those days when he had been property of a studio. This time there were more conditions. At Triumph, he would have to be who they wanted him to be. Raymond looked up to the California sky and considered what going back to the studio would mean. Last time, he'd given up Brick. He'd be giving Brick up again. Brick wouldn't compromise. Brick would never tolerate being the dirty little secret. Signing that contract meant losing the only thing which had ever brought him true happiness. The decision was not that difficult after all. Ray had his answer.

When he got home, he took a nap with Amelia on the couch. The terrier curled up on top of his chest. Being here with Brick and Amelia and Sophie felt so right. He could be himself here. He'd never known who he was before. The joy Ray felt from being in the movies came from playing a role. Ironically, he realized that off screen he finally found a part that brought him fulfillment, one that didn't require a script. This was where he belonged. Ray felt like a stranger everywhere else.

Two hours later, the front door opened. Ray sat up on the couch.

Brick took a seat beside him. "What did Scarno say?"

"He offered me a contract."

"That's great."

Ray shook his head. "You know. It's so strange. The contract was what I was hoping for. I should be on top of the world. But I don't think I can go back. I could feel the knot in my stomach talking with Scarno today. I forgot about the things studios ask their stars to do. I thought I was back for about an hour. I thought I could handle it. We'd figure out what to do. They had marriage and a kid all mapped out for me. All I had to do was sign on the dotted line. Next thing I knew, I was dropping by a tavern without a second thought. I already needed something to cope and the craziness hadn't even started."

"Maybe you didn't know what you were doing."

Ray said he knew all right. "I just didn't think. I forgot to see the repercussions. Maybe it took going back to the studio for me to see that being a star, or anyone other than me, is dangerous."

Brick understood.

"The movie star contract isn't my second chance, my life here with you is. And what we want is more important to me than what the public wants. To blazes with image! I want you. I want this. I want us."

Brick looked confused.

Ray pointed to the contract. "The contract Scarno offered me came with conditions. Plenty of conditions. This had to end so I could date and marry Lorna Chandler. Scarano claimed it would be great publicity for our careers and the studio."

Brick's brown eyes were wide.

"Scarno knew about you. He already knew. He said the truth didn't matter, as long as the public believed the lie."

"Then what's the problem?"

Ray knew Brick was trying to be stoic. Trying to pretend that they could survive those kinds of conditions.

Ray looked him in the eye. "It matters to me. I can't sneak around like that again. I want us to be something more than a secret or a potential source of scandal. I don't want to have to smile with a wife on my arm and pose for *Photoplay* on weekends beside our backyard barbecue. I don't want to return to acting if it means acting full time. For a while, being what everyone envied seemed the most I could hope for, the best I could be. Now I know I can be something better. I've found something more. The price of stardom isn't worth it. Not at all."

Brick lit a cigarette. There were tears in his eyes.

Ray was happy he had his answer. "You're my second chance at life. And this is something I am not willing to risk for anything. I'm going pass on the contract. I was a fool to even consider it. The star system isn't for me. I was Raymond Richmond, movie star, at one time, but I'm not anymore. I'm not willing to make the sort of sacrifice again."

"Are you sure?"

"I've never been more certain of anything in my life." Ray tossed the contract on the coffee table between them and shivered.

"It is getting cold," said Brick. That evening in Los Angeles was unseasonably chilly. He closed the doors onto the patio. "A fog must be rolling in off the ocean."

"I'll make a fire," said Ray. He put some kindling and logs into the fireplace and lit the edge of his contract before slipping in beneath the wood.

Brick met his eyes as the contract was engulfed by the flame. "You sure?"

"I'd better be."

They both laughed.

Ray kissed him. "And everything that I thought mattered didn't really matter that much at all, not in the long run, not with the hiding and the pretending."

Brick leaned back into the couch cushions.

Ray began planting hard kisses across Brick's throat and licking his ears. Brick spoke. "I want tonight to be different." Brick slid to his knees and unbuttoned Ray's fly. "Tonight I want you inside me. I've never had anyone do that. Guess I was playing a role too. I always thought having sex in that way would make me less of a man."

The thought of Brick bottoming excited Ray.

"I want to feel what you feel. Despite everything, I never could trust anyone, not the way I trust you." Brick took Ray into his mouth.

Ray lifted his hips off the sofa. Brick's mouth felt so good. "You sure you want to do this? I don't want to hurt you."

"I'm tougher than I look." Brick licked up the shaft. Lips glistening. "I want to give you something I have never given anyone before."

Ray promised to be gentle.

Brick stopped sucking and stroked him. Rigid. Golden in the light from the hearth. Brick looked into Ray's eyes. "Don't be gentle, just be passionate."

32

When Ray called the next day, Scarno was furious. He
swore Ray would regret his decision. Ray said nothing.
Anything he had to say would only make matters worse.
He kept his mouth closed as Scarno raged. Instead Ray
stared at the new oil painting hanging above the fireplace.
Brick had unveiled his rendering of them late last night.
As Scarno continued to shout into the receiver, the two
men lay naked on the couch. They were much the same
position and state as was captured in oils. Sometimes art
imitates life. Eventually, Scarno's tirade ended and he
slammed down the phone.

Prior to the release of *Beyond the Pale*, the studio did
some heavy editing. Petrovich's contract stipulated a say
in casting, but none in the fate or size of roles. Ray's
billing went from from third to seventh. Much of his
performance ended up on the cutting room floor. Any
hopes Ray had for a resurgence of his career vanished.
Scarno had seen to that. He was a petty man with a score
to settle. Due to the missing footage, the remaining film
was somewhat confusing. *Beyond the Pale* received mixed
reviews and was considered a relatively minor effort in
both Miss Francis's and Mr. Petrovich's careers.

Ray saw the film with Brick when they were on vacation
in San Francisco. The woman at the concession stand said
he looked like an actor in the film. Ray said he'd heard
that before, but told her he wasn't in the film industry.
"I'm too private of a person for that," he said, asking for

extra butter on his popcorn and another Coca-Cola for his friend.

Brick held his hand all the way through the film as well as during the closing credits.

When the film was over Ray turned to him. "I've seen better movies, but never with better company."

Brick smiled at him in the flickering light.

"Besides, it's not really the end at all, now is it?" Ray said, giving Brick's hand a squeeze.

"Nope, there's still another feature."

Owen Keehnen

In addition to his newest novels, The Matinee Idol and Love Underground, writer and historian Owen Keehnen is the author of the humorous gay novel Young Digby Swank, the gay novel The Sand Bar, and the horror novel Doorway Unto Darkness. Keehnen has had his fiction, essays, columns and interviews appear in dozens of magazines and anthologies worldwide and authored the reference book The LGBT Book of Days. He is currently in charge of LGBTQ content for the Chicago tourism website, Choose Chicago. Keehnen is the co-founder and senior biographer of the LGBT organization, The Legacy Project (LegacyProjectChicago.org) which seeks to bring proper recognition to LGBT people and their contributions throughout history. He co-authored Leatherman: The Legend of Chuck Renslow , Jim Flint: The Boy From Peoria, and Vernita Gray: From Woodstock to the White House with Tracy Baim. He is also the author of several M/M ebook novellas for Wilde City. Over 100 of his 1990s interviews with various LGBT authors and activists were collected in the book We're Here, We're Queer. He edited the Mark Abramson memoir For My Brothers and co-edited Nothing Personal: Chronicles of Chicago's LGBTQ Community 1977–1997. He was also a contributor to Gay Press, Gay Power and wrote ten biographical essays for the LGBT history book Out and Proud in Chicago. He was the author of the Starz books (Starz, More Starz, Rising Starz, Ultimate Starz), a four-volume series of interviews with gay porn stars. He has had two queer monologues adapted for the stage, served as co-editor of the Windy City Times Pride Literary Supplement for several years, and was co-founder and former contributor to the horror film website RacksAndRazors.com. He lives in Chicago with his partner, Carl, and his two dogs, Flannery and Fitzgerald. He was inducted into the Chicago Gay and Lesbian Hall of Fame in 2011 and currently serves on the board of the organization.